Guy Ware's first story collection, *You Have 24 Hours to Love Us*, was published by Comma Press in 2012. He is the author of five novels, all published by Salt, including *The Peckham Experiment* and *Our Island Story*. Guy lives with his family in south London.

AF235188

PRAISE FOR *THE FACULTY OF INDIFFERENCE*

'*The Faculty of Indifference* is both funny, diverting, exhausting and baffling all at once. Whatever your tastes, Guy Ware is a writer whose name should be part of the contemporary literary discussion. His is a post-modernism that pushes the past into our increasingly confusing world.'
—Rebekah Lattin-Rawstrone, *Byte the Book*

'Ordinary life is a terrifying prospect in this existential satire about a London spook . . . *The Faculty of Indifference* is a book of dark shadows and dry humour. It's a comedy about torture, death and loneliness, and an existential drama about a world that swirls and twists and turns on us without provocation.' —James Smart, *The Guardian*

PRAISE FOR *THE PECKHAM EXPERIMENT*

★ ★ ★ ★'For all its topical resonance – amid a national housing crisis and the long aftermath of the Grenfell Tower fire – the novel's fatalistic register and taut, controlled narrative voice, by turns doleful and sardonic, set it apart from the preachier political allegories that are currently in such oversupply. Ware's narrator has kept the faith, but he is under no illusions: "the universe is not moral and history has no arc. Its trajectory is an irregular spiral, turning constantly in upon itself . . . If there is an end, a destination beyond mere annihilation, it is lost to sight."'
—Houman Barekat, *The Telegraph*

'Deeply impressive . . . one of the most moving novels I have read in some time.' —KEIRAN GODDARD, *The Guardian*

'Ware is refreshingly sharp on twin psychology . . . featuring a seductively irreverent narrator whose witty, fluid monologue is as Beckettian as it is Steptoe and Son.' —JUDE COOK, *The Spectator*

PRAISE FOR *OUR ISLAND STORY*

'A bizarre, compelling satire reflecting a world where political power takes priority over the "insignificant truth" of climate change.' —KENZIE MILLAR, The Crack

'Ware satirises contemporary Britain . . . where debates and referenda are designed simply to create conflict and hinder action.' —GRANT RINTOUL, *1st Reading*

GUY WARE

A DAY LIKE ANY OTHER

SALT
MODERN
STORIES

SALT

CROMER

PUBLISHED BY SALT PUBLISHING 2026

2 4 6 8 10 9 7 5 3 1

First published in Great Britain in 2026 by
Salt Publishing Ltd
12 Norwich Road, Cromer, Norfolk NR27 0AX United Kingdom

GPSR representative
Matt Parsons matt.parsons@upi2mbooks.hr
UPI-2M PLUS d.o.o., Medulićeva 20, 10000 Zagreb, Croatia

www.saltpublishing.com

Salt Publishing Limited Reg. No. 5293401
A CIP catalogue record for this book is available from the British Library

ISBN 978 1 78463 376 9 (Paperback edition)
ISBN 978 1 78463 377 6 (Electronic edition)

Typeset in Granjon by Salt Publishing

Printed and bound in Great Britain by Clays Ltd, Elcograf S.p.A

For Sophy

Contents

PHILASTER: Oh, but thou dost not know
             What 'tis to die.
BELLARIO: Yes, I do know, my lord:
             'Tis less than to be born; a lasting sleep;
             A quiet resting from all jealousy,
             A thing we all pursue; I know besides,
             It is but giving over of a game,
             That must be lost.
                              —BEAUMONT and FLETCHER,
                              Philaster, or Love Lies a-Bleeding

Tired with all of these, from these I would be gone,
Save that, to die, I leave my love alone.
                              —SHAKESPEARE
                              Sonnet 66

A DAY LIKE ANY OTHER

Confidence Interval

I T WAS NOT yet light, but Annie was awake. She lay on her side of the bed she no longer shared, waiting for the alarm she didn't need. Either there would be a rat – or most of a rat – on the back doorstep when she went downstairs, or there wouldn't. That much was certain. But which? Lately the odds on rat seemed to have been increasing: she'd been finding body parts and sticky viscera staining the flagstones every two or three days. She lived alone, was not a cat person, tolerated no pets at all; but earlier that summer a neighbour's ginger tom had inexplicably set out to woo her with gifts of small birds and field mice. Now, as the air and the leaves began to crisp, his love tokens were becoming meatier, and more frequent.

She made her way downstairs and into the kitchen. She crossed to the fridge and opened it, taking care not to look out through the patio door. She'd need tea before she could face rodents.

So what were the chances? Forty percent?

There'd been no rat yesterday. Did that increase the odds today? At work, David had once tried to explain the difference between dependent and independent events. A tossed coin that had turned up heads a dozen times in a row, he said, was no more or less likely to come down tails next time. She could ask him about it later that morning, if she wanted: he'd be at the management team meeting.

There was a tail, it turned out, still attached to the back half of a rat, its haunches sleek and buttery; there was a head, too, an inch or two apart and set curiously at ninety degrees to the rest of the corpse; and a liver, also neatly separate; the whole collation resembling some fashionably deconstructed meat dish drizzled with a blood jus. There was no sign of the torso. Why would a cat crunch through ribs and forepaws, but leave the liver and the thighs for her?

That was love, she supposed.

On the way to work, between the station and the civic centre, she would pass the Post Office, outside which a queue would be forming already. Opposite the head of the queue, between the phone box and the litter bin, would be a prematurely aged man, yawing like a dinghy on a rolling sea, his protuberant belly half-tamed by filthy braces over a filthy shirt. When he saw her approach, he would stick out his unsteady hand. Or he wouldn't. He wasn't there every day. If today he was, she would drop whatever coins she had in her purse into his hand, and he would shake them gently, as if sifting for counterfeits, as if saying – although he would in fact say nothing – *is that the best that you can do?*

She knew she shouldn't. In her line of work there was a clear policy view on street begging. She should direct him to some suitable agency. But what would that make her? It was Mrs Thatcher who said no one would remember the Good Samaritan if he hadn't had money. Not that she'd ever align herself with Thatcher. Dear God, no. But would we remember the Good Samaritan if he'd handed out cards for the Alcohol Advice line?

In the office, she removed her trainers and slipped into heels.

Julie said, 'Clive's office just rang. He's stuck with the Leader and probably won't make your one-to-one.'

'Probably?'

'That's what they said.'

Which, in this rare case, meant certainly. Which meant she had an hour she wasn't expecting and could read the management team papers after all. Or clear the emails she hadn't cleared last night, when she'd fallen asleep with her iPad on her face. Or both, if she really put her mind to it.

How likely was that?

There was a fat, dog-eared paperback on her desk. She'd once believed that reading a poem before starting work each day would help to clear the mind. Christopher would have spat blood at the idea. But Christopher wasn't here, was he? It was his book, though. Had been his book; it was clotted with his marginalia. *Innocence is no earthly weapon*, she read. Well, possibly. To be honest, she couldn't make much of this one, this poet. God came into it a lot, and history, but most of the time it made no sense at all. She would chuck it, choose another. There was no shortage of poetry.

Christopher. Bearer of Christ.

'You're so predictable,' he'd said, and died. As if anything were more predictable than that.

She fished her iPad from her shoulder bag, opened the

agenda pack and began flicking the pages up through the screen with her thumb, too fast to read. Minutes. Matters Arising. Q2 KPIs. Restructuring the MASH. PA project update. Ofsted preparations. AOB.

PA. Predictive Analytics. David's crusade.

It was ten past nine and already she felt tired.

When she left college and started work, they had family social workers and no computers. They got to know the mums, sometimes the dads. The uncles and the aunts and grannies if they had to. They spoke to teachers, GPs, lollipop ladies. They looked at the children in the round, they said, spotted the signs. That's what they said. Of course, she knew it wasn't true. It was the seventies, for pity's sake. The kids were being raped and battered whether we spotted it or not. Now half the social workers she employed were agency temps who didn't know their colleagues, let alone their clients; they went wherever David's precious algorithms told them to. There were computers everywhere, now, and he was hoovering up all the data he could lay his hands on. School attendance. SATs. Predicted grades. Health records. Library records. Benefits claims. Consumer credit. Rent arrears. Housing repairs. A tenant with repeat repairs to internal doors was highly likely to be a victim – or a perpetrator – of domestic violence. Why? Because Daddy's punching the walls again, that's why. Bloody obvious when you think about it, but they hadn't, had they? It wasn't enough, of course, not on its own. But David said if you pulled all this stuff together you could start to predict who was most at risk. Then you could intervene before it happened.

At which point, someone always said, 'Like *Minority*

Report?' Which was supposed to kill the idea dead, but Annie had never seen *Minority Report*. David would patiently explain why it wasn't like that.

'You can't know for certain,' he always said. 'If you're certain, you don't need a prediction. What we give you is a degree of confidence.' Being David, he meant it in a technical, statistical sense. But these days, Annie thought, they needed all the confidence they could get.

It had been years since she'd met a parent or a child, other than in court.

After the meeting, she ate M&S sushi at her desk.

It had also been years since she'd had lunch with anyone else at work, other than for the purpose of management development.

'You should get out,' Julie said, although she was the one who'd been to M&S. 'You'll be here till all hours with Scrutiny.'

It was true. That afternoon Annie had a meeting with the auditors, then with the MD of a chain of residential care homes; a one-to-one with Geraldine; briefing the Cabinet lead; Scrutiny Committee. She wouldn't leave before ten, wouldn't be home before eleven, where she'd drink a large glass of white wine if the day had been good, a glass of Scotch if it hadn't. Tomorrow she would do the same, or something very like it. She scrolled through the diary on her iPad. It was full for weeks ahead. She could predict now – barring disasters, barring unexpected death, not necessarily her own – where she would be every minute of every working day between now and Christmas.

And the weekends?

'You're so predictable,' Christopher had said, as if it were an insult. It *was* an insult: everyone knew that. He'd been trying to hurt her. He didn't mean he could guess what she would do. He meant he was bored. That she was boring. A woman who could be relied upon to live an exciting, admirable life would never be accused of predictability. It was an insult reserved for people whose choices he could not only foresee, but disdain. Her parents had been predictable. She was predictable. It was nothing but snobbery, really. But honestly, Annie thought, wasn't predictability just another word for consistency? And consistency another word for character?

Shopping and the gym on Saturdays. Rowing, steps, weights; repetitions. Church on Sunday. The Lord be with you. And also with you.

He hadn't *just* died, of course. Not when he said it. But it *had* been the last thing he'd said to her – à propos of what precisely she couldn't now remember – before stamping off to give a lecture on Hardy and collapsing at the lectern, which no one had seen coming. He never recovered consciousness.

A good death? It was certainly quick, for him at least. Annie had to wait a couple of days before the doctors would broach the subject of turning off the machines. They said they'd leave her alone for a while to think. There was no hurry. He wasn't going anywhere. Had that been a little joke?

'Christopher, Christopher,' she had said aloud. 'What have you done now?'

At her desk, a grain of rice stuck to her lower lip. She thought: I will die too. It wasn't a prediction.

As the afternoon wore on, she found herself nodding

without listening to the auditors, allowing the care home manager's words to slip past unattended. It was not unusual. She knew what they were saying, more or less. Probably. David could put a number to it, or a confidence interval, at least, a range within which the true import of their words would fall.

If she could say when she'd die – the minute, the hour, the day or the year, even – that would be a prediction, and it might not be wrong. Prediction was a percentage game, that's what David said. A gambler won't win every time the odds are in his favour, but he has to keep making those bets to come out ahead in the long run. Which was also what Christopher said about the poker he'd played two nights a week for years before he died. Not for the money, Annie thought, but because he thought it gave him a hinterland. It made him feel like David Mamet.

So bloody predictable.

She should have known he would die first, that she would be alone. That was just the way things were. Actuarially speaking. But surely there should have been some years of retirement together first? Holidays in Renaissance cities. Mediterranean cruises. Not cruises. National Trust gardens. Whatever.

Scrutiny Committee was over quicker than she'd feared. There was international football on TV and the members had no desire to string it out. She was home by ten, shoes off, wine poured.

A good day?

Not a bad one, despite the rat. Despite the cat.

And tomorrow? And the day after?

Whatever it says in her diary, she will be alone. And

that will be all right. She will live another twenty years, or thereabouts. She will retire. She will travel and read and pray. She will have good days and bad days, but nothing immoderately awful will happen. She will be happy, sometimes. A few of the children she has worked for will grow up to have lives not unlike hers; most will not. She will die, in due course. Her church professes salvation by grace alone, but manages somehow to stop short of predestination. She will be all right.

Probably.

Finding Himself in a Dark Wood

THE SUN HAD slipped behind the hill and it was already almost dark – as dark as it gets in summer that far north – when Michael finished his first draft and stepped outside for a breath of air. A bat flittered back and forth, dipping between hedges high enough to shelter the cottage from the strong storm winds he could just imagine sweeping off the ocean in winter. Now, though, the air was still; clouds of midges rose and fell around him like smoke in a bell jar, the way at school he demonstrated Brownian motion to bored Year 9s. It was no good standing on the doorstep. He would have to keep moving if he were not to be eaten alive.

Right? Or left?

He chose the path to the left, picking his way carefully down shallow, overgrown steps in the thickening gloom. According to the holiday rental site he'd consulted when the need arose to get away, the cottage *nestled in its own extensive grounds*. In the three days he'd been here, however, he had not ventured beyond the driveway where he'd parked his hired car. Now, on both sides of the narrow, descending track, hedges and shrubs reached across the path above his head to form a tunnel. He felt as if he were leaving the cottage far behind, as if he might emerge into another, less familiar world. One where thirteen-year-olds wanted to learn, perhaps, and did what they were told; where Human Resources Departments were not required; where publishers wanted to publish, readers to read and prize juries to reward the stories he wrote about the unfulfilling lives of bored and disaffected chemistry teachers. But then, in a world where children wanted to learn, would teachers be disaffected? And, if not, what would they write about? Love, he supposed. Or the lack of it. Money. Death. Societal collapse. Was every unhappy chemistry teacher unhappy in his or her own way? He doubted it.

At the end of the path, however, he found himself in the middle of a small, dark wood. Sturdy spruces fifty, sixty feet high, with trunks broader than a man's shoulders – broader than his father, for instance, who had been a giant of a man, given to displays of both colossal strength and incandescent rage – but which nonetheless swayed alarmingly in what seemed to be relatively gentle winds. They were impossible to miss: included prominently in the agency's directions; subsequently filling the view from the window of the second bedroom, which he had adopted as his study. What he had not realized, however, was that the trees lay within the cottage grounds. And yet he had found himself among them without encountering a fence, a gate, or a border of any kind. He thought

– more or less inevitably, he supposed, for a man of his education and temperament – of Dante, of the opening lines of *The Inferno*, in which the poet, having wandered in midlife from the straight path, wakes to find himself in a dark wood. The details did not quite fit. He was thirty-two – not yet, surely, in the middle of his life? He had not wandered from the path: it had simply petered out. Above all, he had not woken here. He had been awake all day, working – all day – on this story. He had stepped outside for a breath of air and found himself, here, in the wood.

Because – there was no way to say this but to say it – there were two of them, two of *him*, there, amid the trees. Himself and another he; not Virgil, not a guide, but himself: Michael. They were in the thick of the wood, where the densely-needled branches overlapped above them, blocking out the lingering radiance of the northern sky. They were both wearing white shirts, however – long sleeves rolled down, cuffs and collars buttoned up against the midges – and each glowed dully in what little light remained. His heart beat wildly and he wrestled down the urge to run inside and bolt the door.

'I'm sorry,' he said, after a while. 'You startled me.'

At the sound of his voice, the other turned away, wrapping his arms around his chest like a straitjacket in the crepuscular gloom.

He said, 'Aren't these woods—'

'Part of the garden?'

The voice sounded more confident than the speaker looked.

'Yes,' he said.

For a while they said nothing. Standing motionless, he'd begun to itch around the hairline. The other scratched his head and said, 'I'm getting eaten alive out here.'

Which is how, shortly afterwards, they found themselves – truly – sitting at the kitchen table, glasses of whisky in hand, trying not to look each other in the face.

So now there were four of them.

At this rate the bottle of whisky, which he'd broached already during his nights alone, would not last long.

He said, 'Who's going down to the village before the shop shuts?'

The one he'd met in the garden – possibly: by now it was getting hard to say – volunteered.

He handed the man a torch and said, 'What's your name, by the way?'

'Mike.'

Of course it was.

Without asking, Mike took the heavy overcoat from the peg on the back of the door and set off down the hill.

'A lot of good in that lad,' one of the others said, after he'd gone.

The fourth disagreed. 'A bit too keen to please. He should stand up for himself.'

Watching the two of them talk was disorienting. Not quite like looking in a mirror, because the images were not reversed. More like watching oneself on CCTV. Did he really look like *that*?

As if aware of his thoughts, they turned to face him.

'So, Michael,' the one on the left said, 'how's it going?'

'All right,' he said. 'Fine.'

The one on the left turned towards the one on the right. 'That's not what we hear, is it, Mick?' He turned back: 'Not why you're here, is it?'

Mick said, 'What is it you do these days, Michael?'

'I teach.'

'*Used* to teach,' said the one on the left. 'Until he was suspended.'

'A misunderstanding. It'll get straightened out.'

'That's not what you wrote yesterday, now is it?'

'You've been reading my notebook?'

'Oh ho,' said Mick, 'does he write?'

'He does indeed. He's not *really* a teacher – are you Michael? I mean, even if he scrapes through the disciplinary, even if there are no criminal charges – which, I have to say, would be a gross injustice – he won't really be a teacher. Deep down, he's a *writer*. Aren't you, lad?'

Mick laughed genially and drained his glass. 'Is he now? And does anybody read what he writes?'

'Only me.'

Michael said that wasn't fair. He'd published at least a dozen stories. He'd been shortlisted for a prize. Plus, he said, the boy should never have left his tent at night. They'd all been told a thousand times.

The two men nodded to each other and refilled their glasses.

'What about you?' he said, trying to get on the front foot. This was his kitchen they were sitting in, after all; the kitchen he'd rented, anyway. His whisky they were drinking. He realized his wallet was in the coat Mike had taken. It looked as though he'd be buying the next bottle, too. 'What makes you both so special?'

Mick gestured to the man beside him. 'Mickey here's a butcher, aren't you, Mickey?'

'I am. I know a thing or two about dead meat.'

'As for me? You could say we're in the same sort of line, Mickey and me. Although, I'm more of a slaughterer.'

Mickey said, 'He's an assassin.'

'He – what?'

'A hired killer. You remember *The Day of the Jackal*?'

Michael did. There'd been a well-thumbed seventies paperback on the shelf at home that must have belonged to his father – their father – or maybe even to *his* father. Gold cover, black lettering, a silhouette of a man in a kepi, his head in the cross hairs. He hadn't enjoyed it much, if he remembered right. Perhaps he'd been too young.

'We all were, lad. But Mick kind of took the whole assassin thing to heart.'

'It's a lot of fun,' Mick said. 'You should try it.'

They were taking the piss. They had to be.

'What about Mike?' he said. 'The other one.'

'You mean the lickspittle kid?'

'Yeah. No.' That didn't seem fair.

'MP for somewhere in south London. Not far from your place, as it happens. Youngest member of the House when he was first elected. I'm surprised you don't remember.'

'You might even have voted for him.'

Michael tried to remember the last election, who his MP was. He thought it might have been a woman, but he couldn't be sure.

'So you see, Michael, you're not really doing fine at all, now are you?'

He didn't think he owed them any more humiliation,

and was determined to wait out the silence that followed. For all he cared, the story could collapse right here. Mick and Mickey seemed unconcerned, and made no effort to break the deadlock. Luckily, there was a knock at the door. Mike Lickspittle, MP, was back with another bottle of whisky, two bottles of wine, a case of beer and a plastic bag full of Styrofoam boxes that turned out to contain four huge portions of chips, three fried cod, a veggie burger and pickled eggs. How he'd hauled it all back up the hill, Michael couldn't imagine. From the pocket of his coat, Mike produced wooden knives and forks, bottles of ketchup, brown sauce and malt vinegar, and a tub of salt.

'I wasn't sure what you might have already,' he said.

'I told you the lad was good for something,' Mick said. 'Apart from target practice.'

'Spending other people's money,' Mickey said. 'He's an MP, after all.'

'What's mine is yours,' Michael said, holding his hand out for his wallet. He'd meant it as a joke, but no one laughed. It wasn't like he had much choice.

When all the food and most of the booze were gone, they drew lots. Michael got to stay in his own bed, but since it was a double, he had to share with Mick.

'Oh great,' he said. 'I'm sleeping with a serial killer.'

'Assassin,' Mick said. 'There's a difference.'

Was there?

'The people I kill are scumbags.'

'I'm sure that's a great comfort to them,' Michael said. 'When they're bleeding out in front of their families.'

Was that a line he could get away with? In a future story, perhaps?

'It's a great comfort to me,' Mick said.

Mickey the butcher got the longest straw – the single bed in what had been Michael's study. It comforted Michael to think Mickey had obviously already read his notebooks. Mike wound up on the sofa in the living room. How that man had ever got to be an MP at twelve, or whatever, was a mystery.

That man, of course, was him.

In the end it was this thought, rather than any fear of Mick's – of his – homicidal expertise, that stopped him sleeping.

There'd been a time – at university, and later, doing his PGCE – when he'd been what might be called a political animal. Student union, demos, out-manoeuvring Trots, all that. His first teaching job, he joined the union, went on strike. Because you did, didn't you? But he never joined the Labour Party – or any party, for that matter – never stood for election. What did he know that everyone else didn't already know? Chemistry? What use would that be in the greater scheme of things? Deep down, he'd always suspected that the people who really believed they could straighten out the world were precisely the sort of lunatics we shouldn't allow anywhere near the levers of power.

Like Mike?

The sort of person who would offer to go down the hill and back, to fetch food and drink for everyone – and remember that Michael was a vegetarian? The sort of person who would happily sleep on the sofa; and who, even now, could be heard downstairs not actually sleeping, any more than Michael was, but tidying up, washing the plates, rinsing out the empty bottles, putting them in the recycling bin.

'Makes you think, doesn't it,' whispered Mick, his mouth in the darkness just an inch from Michael's ear.

'Jesus! Don't do that.'

Mick chuckled.

It's not often you can really call a laugh a chuckle. He'd found it best, in stories, to avoid the word. But that's what it was.

'Mickey's just the same,' Mick said. 'Jumpy.'

Michael hadn't thought he was jumpy. Depressed, maybe, but not nervous. They weren't the same.

'I mean. You being a veggie and all, fair enough. But you'd think he might be made of sterner stuff, being a butcher.'

'Tofu doesn't make you jumpy.'

'No?'

Mick sounded genuinely interested, puzzled even. 'But squeamish, though?'

Michael didn't think he was squeamish, any more than he thought he should be Prime Minister. He'd given up meat a few years ago, he explained, when he was living with Giulia. Giulia, he didn't say, was an Italian teacher, with a precarious toe-hold in post-Brexit Britain; by 'living with' he meant occupying the same one-bedroomed flat their status as teachers had allowed them to buy twenty-five per cent of each in some key worker shared ownership scheme. They'd also shared the only bed for a while before, like Mike, he had relocated to the sofa.

'Giulia was lovely,' he said, 'but didn't love me; our

marriage of convenience proved anything but convenient.'
It was a sentence he'd already used more than once –
including in the story shortlisted for a prize it didn't win.
'The last I heard she was in Argentina,' he said. 'Where,
to be honest, good luck with being vegetarian. My point
being, Mick, that before Giulia, I had no trouble eating
meat, no qualms. I ate veal, for pity's sake: sweetbreads,
black pudding, andouillettes.' In truth, he hadn't just eaten
the stuff, he'd really, positively, *enjoyed* preparing it: skin-
ning rabbits the way his father taught him, spatchcocking
partridge, dicing beef skirt, slicing raw calf's liver, the
texture cool and slippery between his fingers, the blood
that leaked onto his chopping board and dripped onto the
kitchen floor all wiped away without a second thought.
'Giulia changed all that,' he said. When she left, he found
he didn't miss it.

'Still,' Mick said, 'you might think he'd be used to a
bit of death.'

'Death?'

There was a silence. To his surprise, Michael found that
he was disappointed. 'Is that what this is?'

He meant: is that *all* this is? Mick, his preposterous
assassin alter ego leading him by the hand towards the
bright white light? The writer in him revolted. It was
worse than waking up to find it all a dream. Barely worth
the time it would take to scribble down. He knew he
wasn't much of a writer, but surely he was better than
that?

Mick laughed – chuckled – quietly again. 'Oh, no, no,'
he said, 'don't worry. Not death. Not yours, anyway.'

Was that meant to be reassuring?

'Go to sleep, Michael. Things will look different in the morning.'

'Better?'

'Different.'

When we say we didn't get a wink of sleep, we rarely mean it literally, but Michael did not sleep at all that night. Morning, however – sunrise, at any rate – was not long in coming. By four o'clock there was enough daylight leaking through the thin curtains to read his notebooks by, if he hadn't left them in the room next door. Mickey's room, now. Beside him in the bed, Mick the professional killer slept the sleep of the just.

He slipped out from under the duvet. The air was thick with the after-effects of drink, of fried food and pickled eggs. He pulled on his dressing gown and crept downstairs as quietly as the ancient cottage timbers would allow. In the living room, Mike, too, was asleep, his bare feet laid out on the arm of the sofa like a pair of bream on a fishmonger's slab. A regular sound – not a snore, exactly, more a kind of whiffle, the sort of noise a small contented dog might make before a fire – leaked out from under the blanket where the MP's covered head was pressed up against the far end of the sofa.

In the kitchen Michael closed the door and boiled the kettle, cursing the noise it made – like an aeroplane passing overhead, it seemed – but, as far as he could tell, none of his other selves stirred. He made a cup of tea, pulled unlaced boots onto bare feet and slipped out the back door, intending to walk around the house to the bench in the front garden. He would sit and drink and watch the world come awake. Once outside, however, he realized the gross stupidity of this modest ambition. It might be early, but the midges were up and about already, breakfast on their microscopic minds. A dressing gown offered scant protection: he would have to move and keep moving. He squeezed past the parked car, through the gate and out onto the track that led back down to the world. What did all those midges eat, he wondered, when there were no holiday-makers around? Whose blood did they suck?

Once beyond the garden hedges he paused to take in the view. Out of habit, he memorized the details. To his left, the sun had just cleared the hill behind the village, bathing the far side of the loch and the mountains beyond in a rosy glow as clean and bright as pink champagne. In the campsite below him at the foot of the hill a lone figure threaded its way towards the shower block past a rank of dark and silent motorhomes; in an adjacent field, half a dozen jet-black cows, heads bowed, tails flicking lazily, congregated for no obvious reason in the muddiest corner they could find. That would have to do for atmosphere: the midges had caught up with him.

He walked on, following the track down to the road. By turning left, he could make his way into the village, as Mike the MP must have done last night. He turned right. Even if the world were still asleep, he could hardly wander through the village in his dressing gown. To the right, the road led straight uphill, perpendicular to the loch shore, as if built by holidaying Roman soldiers. He had not been up this way before. Sheep, briefly panicked at the sight of him, scuttled across a field of granite rocks and prehistoric bracken.

Whose death, if not his own?

That's what Mick had said, wasn't it? In the night? 'Not yours, anyway.'

He passed a handful of cottages, all set back from the road, up steep narrow tracks that must have been hell to navigate in winter. He had felt the need to get away. Yet here he was, surrounded by mountains.

Why on earth had he chosen to come here?

They were not the same mountains, true – not the same country, even – as the school's Duke of Edinburgh trips he'd always managed to wriggle out of, until earlier that year. Mountains, all the same.

The road came to an abrupt end at a farm gate. Beyond, although there was no path, it would be possible to keep going straight across the boggy patch and up the hill in front of him to where, at the summit, he could see a trig point silhouetted against the delicate pink dawn sky.

'Get in the car.'

Mick's voice. His voice.

'Jesus,' he said. 'Don't do that.'

He turned around. Mick was behind the wheel of the hire car, the window down, a cigarette held out so the smoke drifted upwards. He was wearing a black suit, a black tie, sunglasses. Dressed for work, perhaps. Was this what professional hitmen really wore? Mike and Mickey were in the back seats, also dressed in black.

Mick said, 'You're not exactly kitted out for hill walking.'

He tightened the belt on his dressing gown. The boy had been in his pyjamas.

'Besides,' Mick said, 'we have a funeral to get to.'

Michael shuddered. This was not a good idea: he had

been warned – not that he needed warning – to stay away, to make no contact with the family.

'But, Michael,' said Mike from the back seat of the car, 'he was our father. We *are* the family.'

'Our father?'

'Who else?' said Mickey the butcher. 'What did you think this was all about?

the year of peace

THERE HAD BEEN no rift, no growing sense on either side, he thought, of frustration or annoyance or simple boredom with the other, quite the opposite, and no demand from either that the frequency or pattern of their meetings, which occurred three or perhaps four times a year – never on fixed, predictable dates, except for one, of course, the 26th of July each year, their primary meeting, he liked to think of it   (they liked to think of it, he liked to think)   the pole star of their relationship, as it were   the date they had first met, the anniversary of the succession – the coup, most people would have called it, if they had heard of it – the palace revolution, say, that brought the current ruler of her father's country to power almost half a century ago, in place of the current leader's father, who had himself ruled for almost fifty years, whose fathers had been sultans as long as there had been a sultanate, and who, once deposed, was neither executed nor imprisoned but exiled, if exile is the term – retired, perhaps – not unnaturally, to this country, his country, the country that had, in reality, ruled the sultanate throughout, appointing its ministers, its diplomats, its political advisers and armed forces, and had, in fact, been waging war against rebels in the south of the country on the sultan's behalf for several years, including the year of 1968 – still known by some amongst his country's military as "the year of peace", not because of the White Album or the events in May, much less the assassinations or the Tet Offensive, but because, erroneously, they believed it to have been the one and only year of the war-scarred twentieth century in which they had not been deployed on active duty some-where across the globe – although try telling that to the survivors of the bombing raids, of the burnt villages, burnt crops and poisoned wells, or to the victims of mass arrest and torture, he said, or rather wrote, in the book he called *The Year of Peace*, and published, not coincidentally, with a launch party on the 26th of July, in a Piccadilly bookshop, forty-four years to the day after the coup, or succession, at which she had listened to him lecture the small audience briefly about the geo-political significance of events in her father's country to his country and its allies, before reading a brief extract from the book and speaking a little about his reasons for writing it, which were only partly professional, as an historian, and partly personal, related to his own father's involvement in the events the book described, the coup and the war no one ever spoke about – including his father, who always described himself as a civil servant, and whose story he only discovered after he had died – and when he finished speaking and his publisher invited people to drink more wine and ushered him towards a table piled with copies of his book to sign, she picked one up, holding back while other customers, more eager for signatures, approached, and flipped through the pages, allowing the queue to dissipate before she stepped up to the table and said

I'm only here as a result of that coup

here in London?

that too   she said   her father like his father had worked for the old sultan, but unlike his father had stayed loyal and followed him into exile, or retirement, here, helped him settle, here, and when the sultan died, she said, two years later, he stayed because he'd met a woman, my mother, and there you have it, I am here, she smiled and   he, not knowing what else to say, asked if she would like him to sign her copy of the book, and she said yes   and told him her name, for the dedication, she knew his, of course, and had no need to ask him for his phone number, but did so anyway   and

they met, again

for a drink, although she did not drink, and then dinner – yes, she said, don't worry, I do eat – and while they ate they talked about her country, mostly, which was not her country really, she said, she was not born there, her mother did not come from there, and she had only visited as a tourist – surely more than that? he said – a tourist, okay, with plenty of relatives to visit, and stay with, mostly in the capital, she said, although also aunts and cousins in the second city, in the south, the city where, as his book revealed, the old sultan's second palace had been home to one hundred and fifty of his five hundred slaves who were women, she paused   and looked at him, he saw her eyes were black, so black it was difficult, in the low light of the restaurant, to tell where the pupils ended and the irises began, and he knew that she knew that he wanted

to ask if her aunts had been amongst the one hundred and
fifty female slaves, living in the palace in the city that had
been surrounded by the rebels, although never captured
but wouldn't, not yet   and instead he talked about
the Global Slavery Index that suggested there were still,
or now, almost twenty-six thousand slaves in her country,
her father's country, which it turned out she did know,
although there were problems with the methodology, she
said, that made the number questionable at best – just like
the equivalent number for his country, which was over
eight thousand – she was not excusing slavery or attacking
his country, which was also her country, she reminded
him, where she'd been born, where she'd grown up and
lived almost all her life – almost? he said, grasping for
distraction, for a way off the hook, and she   paused
long enough to let him know she was choosing whether
to be distracted, to let him down gently   then said
she'd lived in the States, in Cambridge, Massachusetts for
a few years – studying? he asked – and she agreed, yes, a
masters that turned into a PhD but along the way I got
involved in Obama twenty oh-eight and spent a couple of
years in Washington, and   he wondered, not for the
first time, what she was doing here at all, with him, but
asked why she'd come back, here, to London and   after
a moment she said

    to get married

    which luckily she said while he still had his fork raised,
having just taken a mouthful of fish, which allowed him
to pretend a bone had caught in his throat, necessitating
several coughs and sips of water and the ingestion of a
wholly unnecessary pellet of bread before he said – and

what does your husband do? – and

she threw back her head and laughed like a drain   not like a drain, like nothing he had ever heard   she threw back her head and a strand of black hair worked loose from her headscarf as her shoulders rocked and the blackness of her hair, the whiteness of her teeth and the scarlet of her lips and throat reminded him, incongruously, of revolutionary art, of Bolshevik posters and the Spanish Civil War, while the sound was guttural   not guttural, visceral the sound was shocking, physical and intimate, timeless and elemental, like magma churning the earth's core, he thought, like God, and, like God, her mercy was infinite when she said I'm sorry, he's an academic, an economist, but it didn't work out, he left me standing at the altar and – before he could worry about asking how that worked, wasn't it the man at the altar, waiting, but perhaps it was different, for them? – she said   that's just a figure of speech, actually he left me in his flat and moved into the hotel we'd booked for the reception, we met in the lobby the next day and decided it was for the best, we'd return the gifts and   he relaxed and I relaxed and we spent a very pleasant evening together, but   what about you, are you married? and he said

no, I mean, I was, that didn't work out, either and there was a pause, a silence they could both hear, while the waiter took away their plates and asked if they would like desserts, and later, when he saw her into a cab and asked if he could see her again she said of course, call me, but when he did her phone diverted straight to voicemail, more than once   until

she called him   three or four months later, and said,

I'm sorry, I meant to call, I've been really tied up, how are
you? and when she said, do you want to have dinner again?
and he said   yes,   she said, tonight?   and
even though he'd been planning to write a book review he
should have written a month ago, he said   yes   and
when, after they'd eaten, she asked if he would like to come
to her hotel room, he said   yes   and that became
the pattern, she'd call, every few months, he'd never know
when to expect it, couldn't expect it, except the 26th of July,
the anniversary of the coup without which she wouldn't be
here   he kept the day free   but otherwise he never
knew when she would call and in between he'd call her
sometimes, not often, knowing that she wouldn't answer,
that he would leave a message, to share his news and let
her know he was still alive and never to say he loved her,
and he found, to his surprise, it suited him   perfectly
he wanted nothing more   until

one afternoon, in the middle of a meeting at his publisher's offices, a meeting after which he feared they might no
longer be his publishers, his mobile rang and he answered
it there, in the meeting   because he wouldn't get a
second chance   he said his name and a voice – not her
voice, a man's voice – said, I'm sorry to disturb you, but you
should know that she is dead

bad news? the publisher's assistant asked, are you all
right? – but   there was an accident, the man's voice said,
she died last night, and

it isn't hard to find where somebody is buried if you
know the date, the name, the faith of the recently deceased,
but still he put it off for over a month, he was so busy, he
had a day clear in his diary soon, the 26th of July, he'd go

then, he didn't know if he should buy flowers, if that would be appropriate, culturally, but   when he found the cemetery, the garden of peace, when he found her grave, the earth was still black and moist around the edges of the granite kerb   the signs of disturbance were still evident there was a low plain black stone, no more than a foot high, with her name, her dates and an inscription he could not read, in front of which, in a simple vase, stood a fresh rose, deep red, almost scarlet against the black stone and white lettering, and he thought of her mouth, of her laugh and grabbed the rose and tore the petals from it, scattering them over nearby graves   then picked them up, carefully, and dropped them in a litter bin before he left and

it was petty   and

he regretted it   and

later, that night, that September, that Christmas, the following July, he hoped   he didn't hope   that when he returned, after a year, each year, to the garden of peace, to her grave, he would find another rose he hadn't brought himself

The Long Hall

M Y FATHER ALWAYS called it the "gallery". I argued
that a gallery was a room – or a set of rooms – dedicated to the display of visual art. What we had was more of
a hall, or corridor, or even a passageway. My father would
remind me that it contained pictures, which was true
enough: there were seven, all selected for their historical
relevance, along with a polished suit of armour and a bust
of Sir Philip Sidney. But nobody went there for the art, I
said: although old, the paintings were not good, and merely
filled what would otherwise be blank spaces on the walls
between the four windows on the left-hand side of the
passageway and the four doors on the right, plus the final
door, at the end, which faced me as I entered the hall, or
corridor, each morning, shortly after breakfast. The view
of the formal gardens from the windows was likewise
pleasant enough, but there were better. From my father's
bedroom on the floor above, for example, one could see
not only the gardens, but over the wall, with its espaliered
apricot trees, to the countryside beyond.

As Tudor architecture was my father's area of expertise, however, I dare say he was right, if only technically,

although contemporary documents suggest the original inhabitants referred to it as "The Long Room". This seemed to me no better than "gallery": it was certainly *long* – six or seven times longer than it was wide – but it was clearly not a *room*. It was not a place one visited or would wish to spend time. No, it was neither a gallery nor a room, but a hall, a corridor, a passageway to the actual rooms that lay behind the four doors to the right, and, I suppose, behind the door at the end, facing me; also to the vast linen press that occupied the space between the second and third windows on the left, where otherwise an eighth picture – most likely another portrait of another minor Seymour or Howard – would have hung.

The presence of the linen press was something of a mystery. Its gleaming, finely carpentered, beaded and polished walnut finish was so obviously Georgian, not Tudor. Indeed, it was the only significant item of furniture in the house that dated from later than 1603 – apart from the beds. My father insisted on the importance of a good night's sleep, to the lack of which he attributed Henry VIII's persistent marital difficulties. We might have had to sit – to eat, to read, or simply to avoid further motion – on some of the most unaccommodating chairs and benches outside of a railway waiting room, but we slept in comfort. And after each untroubled night, I would rise, wash, dress and descend to the dining room for breakfast, after which I would proceed to the hall, or corridor, and there the linen press would be, gleaming, out of time, and locked.

When my father died, I expected the key to the press to pass to me, along with those to all the other doors, safes, caskets, padlocks, cupboards, clocks and trunks that festooned the house and its outbuildings. For as long as I could remember, these keys had been corralled, by size, on three brass rings, threaded on a braided silk rope that served my father for a belt. It may in fact have *been* a belt – for a dressing gown, perhaps, or a velvet smoking jacket – but my father used it to prevent his trousers – which had all become two or three sizes too large for his emaciated frame – from sliding into a puddle around his ankles. But when his solicitor – a thin, nervous man who said 'sorry' far more often than he meant it, and coughed whether or not he had a cold, and who was now, I supposed, *my* solicitor – passed me the three brass rings, along with the deeds to the house and divers other official documents, he assured me that these, and only these, were the keys that had been in my father's possession at the moment of his untimely breakdown and subsequent death.

The following morning, I passed as usual from the dining room into the hall, or corridor. I ignored the view from the first and second windows to my left, and the temptations of the first and second doors to my right – which I knew led respectively to the schoolroom (with which I had been familiar from the age of five) and the library (which I first entered a few years later). Without once looking ahead to the door at the end of the hall, or passageway, which faced me, I approached the linen press, keen to discover what additional inheritance it contained. One by one I tried each of the keys, starting with the smallest and working my way up to those I knew without having to hold them up to the lock were far too large, but trying them anyway. None fitted.

The next day, along with the keys, I brought a hammer,

a chisel and a brutal, heavy iron bar bent at each end in opposite directions, both flattened, one split, like a viper's tongue. My father had called it a 'jemmy', and used it to open packing cases, to prise items of interest out of the clay when the moat dried in summer, and as a weapon with which to threaten me. To make it easier to carry everything, I tied the braided silk rope, with the three brass key rings hanging from it, around my waist.

I had thought that the hammer and chisel – or, if not them, the jemmy – would make short work of the recalcitrant lock. However, when it came to the crunch, so to speak, I could not bring myself to damage the fine inlay work, or to splinter the doors. The press might be out of place in the corridor, or passage, of a moated pre-Reformation manor house, but it was nonetheless a thing of beauty and considerable craftsmanship. Besides, I thought how foolish I would feel if, after destroying it, the press turned out to contain only *linen*. This seemed unlikely, but I still decided to effect a feint and, in place of frontal assault, to attack the problem from the rear. I thought it likely that the back of the press might not be finished to the same high standards as the front and sides, and might therefore be susceptible to burglarization with minimal force and limited damage – which damage could be easily hidden by replacing the press against the wall. So I sauntered – as far as it is possible for a man carrying a heavy iron bar, bent at the ends, a hammer and a chisel, to saunter – past the press, as if making my way to the third or even the fourth door of the hall, or corridor, before turning suddenly back on myself and coming swiftly at the press from the far – the right-hand – side. Only then did I notice that it was not, in fact, flush with the wall, but stood about an inch and a half away from it. This made it easier for me to get my right hand behind, and push, while lifting with my left as best I could. Slowly, and with considerable effort, I managed to shift the heavy press, pivoting it around its rear left foot.

Once the press stood at forty-five degrees to the wall, and I had more than enough space to get behind it with my hammer and chisel, or even the jemmy, it became obvious that the rear, whilst unvarnished, was no less sturdily built than the front and sides. Before I could decide what to do, however, my eye was caught by something on the wall itself. At just the spot where the face of another Seymour, or another Howard, might have hung if the press itself had not occupied the space between the second and third windows, was a large and fleshy mushroom. The upper surface was soot grey, the gills below shivered pearlescent and soft; it measured six inches across and protruded from the wall by an inch and a half. With my chisel I detached it with as little damage as I could – although it was impossible to say how much of the fungus remained, embedded in the wallpaper, or in the ancient plaster and brickwork beneath. I recalled having read somewhere that what we describe as mushrooms are just the visible "fruit", as it were, of vast invisible fungal networks, capable of extending and, in a sense, communicating, over immense distances.

Abandoning my tools where they lay, and leaving the linen press akimbo, I retraced my steps, carrying the mushroom carefully out of the hall, or gallery, and upstairs into what I thought of as my father's study, although it was now of course *my* study. I placed my trophy in an empty cigar box of the sort my father, once he had smoked the contents, used to store cufflinks, loose change, watches, interesting pebbles, letters, knick-knacks, corkscrews, nail clippers and all the assorted paraphernalia of adult life. Consulting his field guide and comparing its images and information with that obtained from the internet, I concluded that the mushroom was edible, or at least not poisonous. And that evening, I ate it – sliced and fried and incorporated in a three-egg omelette – along with a light salad and a white Bordeaux from the lower, more valuable racks of my father's cellar. The taste – of the mushroom, not the wine – was a little musty, but not unpleasant. The wine was excellent.

That night, however, I woke in the small hours with violent, stabbing pains in my belly and an irresistible urge to shit. Not bothering with a dressing gown, I raced to the bathroom, making it just in time to void my bowels in the toilet and not, as I had feared, on the floor or, worse still, all over myself. I had to return twice more before daybreak, and once after, following which I crawled back to bed, weak, shivering, my face clammy with cold sweat, in no state to face breakfast. It could have been the wine, I thought, but it seemed unlikely. I spent the day in bed, and – feeling too unwell for self-abuse – in prayer.

The following day I woke early – hungry and with greater energy, fully purged of whatever poison I had ingested. After a substantial breakfast, I returned to the hall, or corridor, and, without any pretence of interest in the view from the windows, or in the rooms beyond the third and fourth doors, or even the door at the end, which faced me, I approached the linen press directly. It stood, not as I had left it, at forty-five degrees to the wall, but parallel to it, albeit at a distance of about two inches. Once again, by pushing with my right hand while lifting with my left, I was able to pivot the press far enough away from the wall to gain access to its rear, which I now intended to break open with my hammer and chisel, or jemmy, as necessary. Once I had rotated the press sufficiently to allow the light in, however, I saw immediately that, where previously the mushroom I had eaten (and then regretted eating) had grown, there were now *two* mushrooms, each larger than the first, at about eight inches in length and standing proud of the wall by a good two inches. Uncertain as to their degree of toxicity, but forewarned by experience, I decided not to handle the fungi directly. Having no receptacle to hand, I removed my shirt, laid it carefully against the skirting behind the press, then carefully chiselled the new growths away from the wall. I wrapped them securely in my shirt before carrying the package out and depositing it in the fire pit where my father burned waste that could not be more effectively recycled. Crossing the garden, I passed the outhouse he used to store lawnmowers, shears, secateurs, spades, forks, bamboo poles, plant pots, trowels, compost, rat traps, fertilizer, twine, *et cetera*; it occurred to me that, among the slug pellets and aphid sprays, I might find a specialist fungicide. I was right: not only was there such a chemical, but also a dispenser ideal for my purpose: a plastic tank one straps to one's back attached via a length of flexible pipe to a triggered nozzle designed to give an accurate dose of poison in aerosol form. I immediately poured a healthy slug of fungicide into the tank, diluted it with water, according to the instructions, strapped it to my shirtless back and tested the apparatus on the two mushrooms I had not yet disposed of: they shrivelled with satisfying speed. I returned at once to the gallery where I found that, in the short time since I had left, four more mushrooms had begun to sprout on the wall behind the linen press. I sprayed, and watched as they, too, died.

At this moment, I was startled by a heavy thump and the sound of splintering wood to my right. I turned and saw that the fourteenth-century Italian portrait of St Antony of Padua preaching to the fish at Rimini, which occupied the space between the third and fourth windows, had crashed to the floor, smashing beyond repair one corner of its sixteenth-century frame. On the wall where it had always hung was the largest mushroom I had yet seen. I sprayed it liberally, and watched it die.

It occurred to me that, although I could see no further sign of fungal growth, it was better to be safe than sorry: I would spray the walls behind each of the pictures in the hall. I proceeded therefore up past the fourth window, where I removed the small, school-of-Holbein portrait of John Seymour (brother of Henry VIII's third wife), propped it against the skirting, and dosed the wall behind. A little further up, on a pedestal in the corner to the left of the door at the end of the hall, or corridor, stood the bust of Sir Philip Sidney, behind which I also sprayed, for good measure.

I now found myself having penetrated further into the hall, or corridor, than I ever had before – standing more or less face-to-face with the door at its end, which, it occurred to me, I could now open. Even if it were locked, the key would no doubt be found on one of the three brass rings that hung from the braided silk rope around my waist.

But, no: duty called. I would first complete my task. Accordingly, I crossed in front of the last door, sprayed behind the suit of armour, behind the still life – or *nature morte,* as my father preferred – by Hans Memling; I then stepped backwards, admiring my handiwork, to the wall past the fourth door, where I took down Edward Howard, uncle to both Anne Boleyn and Catherine Howard, second and fifth wives respectively of the sleep-deprived king. As I sprayed the wall, the third door opened and I heard a woman's voice call my father's name, that is, *my* name: Mr Perceval. I hesitated; the voice repeated the name, adding: 'Please step this way.'

Passing through the third door for the first time, I found a middle-aged woman – short; with a plump, not unfriendly face; and soberly dressed – holding out her hand for me to shake. Behind her, a room far larger than I would have expected was filled with desks arranged in clusters of four or six, each desk equipped with a computer, a lamp, a coffee mug, files and an assortment of plants and small, plush toys. At each desk sat a man or a woman. There were no windows: lights set into the ceiling tiles illuminated the room. The effect was bright, but antiseptic.

'Good afternoon, Mr Perceval.'

I switched the fungicide spray from my right hand to my left and shook hers. She directed me to a chair on the far side of her own desk, which had no computer or files.

'I see you found us all right?'

I sat down; the fungicide tank banged awkwardly against the back of the chair, forcing me to perch on the edge of the seat. She invited me to take off the appara-tus. Thanks to my father's rigid tastes, however, I was no stranger to uncomfortable furniture; I politely declined. Apart from the tank and its straps I was naked from the waist up.

'So, Mr Perceval, what do you know about St Antony?'

'Of Padua?' I said, recalling the portrait that had fallen from the wall.

'Or Lisbon, if you prefer. Same feller.'

It came to me. 'He was the patron saint of lost things.'

'*Is*, Mr Perceval. The saints are eternal; he helps us still to find those precious items – including people – that we may have mislaid. What else?'

'He preached by a river, and the fish came up to listen.'

'Very good, very good. And do you know how he died at all?'

I had no idea. I hazarded a guess that he might have been executed for his faith. Burned at the stake, perhaps?

'Not at all, Mr Perceval, although not wholly wrong. Do you know what St Antony's Fire might be?'

Again, I was at a loss.

'It is the popular name for ergotism. I won't ask if you know what *that* is; suffice to say it has nothing to do with an overly high opinion of oneself, or an excessive fondness for logical deduction!' She paused to permit herself a chuckle at her own puns, before continuing more soberly. 'It is a condition, Mr Perceval, from which the saint himself suffered. It causes a sort of dry gangrene, mostly in the hands and feet, identified through peeling skin, loss of sensation and, in time, decay of the affected organs. It causes also convulsions – painful seizures and spasms, along with diarrhoea, nausea, headache, itching and strange prickling sensations under the flesh, sometimes giving rise to the delusion of infestation by invisible creatures. Eventually, it causes mania, psychosis and death.'

Throughout this litany of symptoms, I had been nodding along: when it ended, I found myself with nothing to say.

'It is caused,' she said, 'by the ingestion of rye or other cereal contaminated by a fungus . . .'

'A mushroom?'

'Not exactly; but, again, not unrelated. The culprit is an ergot fungus: tiny, but not invisible: *Claviceps purpurea.*'

'Purple . . . club . . . head?'

'Exactly so, Mr Perceval. And they wouldn't have called it that if they couldn't see the little purple buggers, now, would they?'

'I suppose not.'

'Good. Good. Well,' she said, standing up again, 'I think that's everything. We'll see you tomorrow morning at nine.'

I stood up and she held out her hand again. I said, 'Nine?'

'O'clock, Mr Perceval. Sharp.'

I shook her hand again. Back in the hall, or corridor, I was pleased to see that the walls I'd sprayed had dried without leaving any stain. I replaced the pictures in the order I had removed them, starting with St Antony, with its damaged frame, and proceeding clockwise to Edward Howard. I then went on to complete the task – removing each remaining picture in turn, spraying the wall behind and then replacing it – beginning with the picture between the third and second doors and continuing clockwise until I returned to the linen press, which I set straight against the wall, and left.

The following morning, after a brisker than usual breakfast, I returned. The pictures all lay at uneven angles on the floor, with varying degrees of damage. The suit of armour lay in a tangled heap, its silver polished plates scattered around the bust of Sir Philip Sidney. From each wall, between each window and each door, from each corner, there sprouted a mushroom, the largest of which must have been two feet across. I saw that I would have to remove them, and fetched my chisel and an old decorator's dustsheet that had been left for many years in a cupboard outside the kitchen, which I could use to catch and wrap the fungi as I scraped them from the walls. My shirt would be far too small this time: besides, I had an appointment at nine, and did not want to present myself half-dressed again. The thought prompted me to check my watch: it was already a few minutes to the hour. I could not possibly chisel off all the mushrooms, clear them away and re-hang the pictures before I was due in the room behind the third door. And yet, I could not possibly leave the hall, or corridor, or even passageway, in this state. I worked as fast as I could, but it was nearly ten by the time I wiped my hands on my trousers, straightened my hair and knocked at the third door.

There was no answer.

I returned to the kitchen, and thence to the garden, where I burned my crop of mushrooms in the fire pit, standing upwind to avoid any noxious smoke they might emit. There was no smoke, however, except that from the kindling I had used to set the fire; the mushrooms themselves burned like gas with a clean, iridescent flame, and left no ashes.

The following morning, skipping breakfast altogether, I set off to the gallery before eight: if the mushrooms had re-grown, I would have time to clear them away before nine o'clock. When I arrived, I found each of the pictures, the armour and the bust once again on the wooden floor, with evidence of progressive damage. Where before there had been single mushrooms, there were now clumps – troops? clouds? schools? – of innumerable grey fungi, some up to three feet across. By dint of considerable effort, however, I was able to chisel them all off the walls and into the dustsheet, which I left, knotted at the corners, beside the linen press; and, if not to re-hang the pictures, at least to stand them against the skirting where I hoped they would come to no further harm. I brushed myself down, wiped the sweat from my brow and presented myself at the third door just as my watch's second hand swept up to join the minute hand in pointing to the hour.

This time the door opened promptly. Behind it, however, in place of the kindly woman I had previously spoken to, there stood a young man barely older than I. His suit was much too small: tight across the belly and under the arms, the trousers petering out well above the ankle to display a disconcerting acreage of white sock. His beard, too, seemed too small for his face, stretched thin and tight across his broad cheeks until it was possible to see the flesh beneath, its edges carved with artificial precision.

'Yes?'

I explained why I had come, why I had not come yesterday, and hoped that I could start again, today. The young man showed no sign of interest, and every sign of impatience. The moment I paused, he jerked his thumb to the right, said 'Next door, dumbass,' and slammed the door shut in my face.

Even without the gesture I would have been in no doubt that he meant not the second door, behind which lay the library, but the fourth, through which I had so far never ventured. He could not, of course, have meant the last door, facing me at the end of the long hall, or corridor. No reasonable interpretation of his words could be taken as an instruction to bypass, as it were, the fourth, and proceed directly to the final door.

When I knocked on the fourth door, however, there was no response. The key would be on one of the brass rings on the knotted silk rope, which at that moment hung, not around my waist, but from a hook on my bedroom wall. Turning to fetch it, I noticed the makeshift sack of mushrooms I had been forced by lack of time to leave knotted up beside the linen press. If I were going to leave the corridor, or passageway, I should take it with me, and dispose of the mushrooms before returning with the keys. Once outside, however, I discovered a light rain had begun to fall; it would be futile now to attempt to light a fire. Waiting for the shower to pass, I realized that – having missed breakfast – I was hungry; I made toast and scrambled two eggs while the rain beat against the window. By the time I had washed up my plate and scoured the pan, to which so much of the egg stuck fast, and once I had managed to light a fire with the damp kindling and had disposed of that day's mushrooms, it was nearer to noon than nine, and surely too late to present myself at the fourth door. I returned to my bedroom, where I read and masturbated until dinnertime.

The following day was Sunday, which I spent as usual in contemplation of my sins, and of His divine mercy.

On Monday, I rose at five, breakfasted hurriedly and made my way to the gallery. There, I cleared away countless mushrooms, hauling three dustsheet-sacksful out to the garden and burning them in turn, before returning via the bathroom, where I washed my hands and face and brushed my hair. Finally, I presented myself before the fourth door at nine o'clock sharp.

There was no answer.

I hastened back to my room, collected the silk rope with the three brass rings holding all the keys I had inherited from my father and returned, at a run, to the gallery, or hall, or corridor, and straight to the fourth door, despite noticing, in passing the first and second doors, that already grey fungi were beginning to reappear. They were tiny now – perhaps invisible to anyone unused to dealing with them – but how large and numerous would they become by the time I completed whatever appointment awaited me behind the fourth door? It was a risk that I would have to take. I fumbled through the keys, trying each in turn, mixing them up and having to start all over again several times before, finally, a large, complex iron key that, unlike many of the others, showed no trace of rust, slipped silently into the lock, and turned.

'Good morning,' said a young woman in a pale blue tunic from behind a reception desk. 'Do you have an appointment?'

I explained that I had been told to come at nine o'clock; that I had been invited, or instructed, to come the previous week, but that this had proved impossible; the delay had been unavoidable, but I hoped it would not matter.

The young woman requested some personal details, which I provided. She made no notes, however, merely checked my answers against those already displayed on the computer screen in front of her. Finally, she asked me to take a seat, said she would see what they could do, and disappeared through a door immediately behind her desk. Behind me I found a row of hard plastic chairs, each occupied by a man or a woman, reading, scratching or staring at the wall where a TV set broadcast a property renovation programme with the sound turned off. After ten minutes or so, the woman reappeared and I stepped forward expectantly. She motioned me away, however, and called another name. An elderly man at the end of the row stood up and left the reception area through a second door I had not previously noticed. The young woman indicated to me the now vacant seat before disappearing once again through the door behind her desk.

On TV, a middle-aged couple appeared delighted with the changes to their home.

Finally, the young woman in the pale blue tunic reappeared and summoned me to the reception desk. 'I'm sorry, Mr Perceval, but there's nothing we can do.'

I explained again that the delay, while superficially my fault, really had been unavoidable.

'I'm sorry,' she repeated. 'It's too late.'

'Too late?'

'There's really nothing we can do.'

I left. It was not her fault. It was not anybody's fault. Back in the gallery, the mushrooms had grown thickly over the walls, the ceilings and the edges of the floor. St Antony, the Seymours, the Howards and the still life were all where I had left them, propped against the skirting, but had now been entirely swallowed up by fungi; and even from where I stood, at the fourth door, it was no longer possible to see the end, the last door, the one at the end of the long hall that had faced me, every morning as I entered, after breakfast, on my way to somewhere else.

Point and Shoot

GREEN PILL, RED pill, white pills: done. For now.

Rain trickled down the still-black window. Thirty minutes before he could even make a cup of tea. These new white pills. What was he supposed to do for half an hour?

What Rob did – what he used to do – no one did any more. Not that it was difficult or required any particular skill. It was just . . . an approach . . . a way of fixing the world. Not mending it, he didn't mean that. More like setting, crystallizing, the way photographers used dark-room chemicals to fix an image that would otherwise smear softly under your thumb.

No one did that any more.

Point and shoot. That's what they called simple cameras, ones any fool could use. Before cameras were all mobile phones anyway.

Point and shoot.

That wasn't it, either. Photography. That wasn't what he was talking about. It was just . . .

It was time enough. He warmed the pot, swirling the water before tipping it out into the sink. The small pot; no use for the big one, now. He spooned loose leaves – one, one-and-a-half teaspoons – and re-boiled the kettle.

It wasn't hard. It was just not wanted.

Not Wanted On Voyage. Where had that come from?

He saw her, sometimes, still, heard her more often: a voice, distinct, brooking no misunderstanding – that was Carol, all right – calling from a room he had just left.

He poured a mug of tea, cut two thick slices and dropped them into the toaster that could take four. The condemned man. The words came, now. The condemned man ate a hearty breakfast, that's what they always said. Years since anybody hanged, but still, they said it.

Tea, toast. What else? Butter – the doctor wouldn't like that. Fuck him. Marmalade. Ditto, he supposed. It was always going to be something, wasn't it? The difference was that Rob knew what, precisely. A bit of fat and sugar wouldn't alter that.

You didn't have to see a GP any more, didn't have to look them in the eye. Repeat prescriptions. Two months' supply, just click on your phone and collect it from the pharmacy. They'd even deliver, but he preferred the walk. Even on days like this, with the rain spitting in yesterday's puddles. He was slow, but so what? You could shave a week or two each time: no one counted. The woman in the chemist's was usually friendly, if there wasn't a queue. She never asked to see his card, the one for free prescriptions because he had a lifelong condition. She said he was in their system, and little by little his stockpile grew.

Lifelong could cover a multitude of sins.

They had agreed, he and Carol: they would help each other, if it came to that. They would fix it for each other.

Alistair was behind the bar at the Prince of Denmark, which he wasn't always, not at lunchtime. He nodded to Rob while scraping the head off a Guinness for another customer. Young lad. Hair like pissed-on snow, with a tuft sticking up where a fringe should be. Rob hadn't seen him in the Prince before. The lad took his Guinness over to a table by the window, shrugged off a small rucksack and a padded coat. That was all right. Alistair had to get new customers somehow.

'Christ's sake, Rob. Not on the bar.' Alistair was pointing at the paper bag. It was white with big green crosses either side. 'Anyone would think you're dealing.'

Rob laughed. 'Who to? Tintin over there?' All the same, he took the bag off the bar and squeezed it into his overcoat pocket. He felt the cardboard packets give way under the pressure.

He used to think he'd pulverize them – Carol's spice grinder would be just the job – and dissolve the powder. Tie a tourniquet around his arm and – bang! Point and shoot.

That was stupid, though. Too much TV. Where would he get a big enough syringe? He'd want a turkey baster.

They hadn't exactly agreed. He'd offered, and Carol had said all right, if it ever came to it, maybe just to shut him up, stop him talking while she tried to watch TV.

Alistair was pouring his pint now. 'How's things?'

'Oh, you know.'

Things were much the same. Which was surely the point of things. Stability. Also: getting in the fucking way.

Alistair reached between the pumps to place the pint in front of him. 'You want a short with that?'

He could wash them down with whisky. No, not whisky – too much of that would make him sick. Which wouldn't help. A really nice bottle of wine, perhaps? It wasn't like he'd have anything better to spend his money on. Champagne'd be too fizzy. He giggled, as if he'd been drinking already. He shook his head. If beer made you queer and whisky made you frisky, what was it wine did?

Wine made you fine, that was it.

Fine.

Point and shoot.

'No,' he said. 'You're all right.'

He handed over a fiver, told Alistair to drop the change in the bottle. Not that there'd be much. Good job he wasn't trying to drink himself to death.

'There's a paper there,' Alistair said. 'If you're bored.'

'Thanks.'

Bored. That was about the truth of it. Was he in severe pain? No. Had the doctors given him six months to live? No, more's the pity. If he had that he could go to Switzerland. If he had that and the money.

He took the paper and his pint over to a table across from where the young lad with the hair was wiping off a Guinness moustache with his sweatshirt sleeve.

The paper turned out to be the *Daily Express*. He wasn't that bored. Rob laughed to himself again. A little chuckle, but out loud. He should get a grip of that, he thought, before people went thinking he was happy.

'There is something funny?'

It was Tintin. His voice was flat, hard to read. He surely wasn't trying to pick a fight? It was eleven a.m.; there were only the two of them. Alistair had disappeared wherever barmen go when they aren't actually behind the bar. Daylight leaked stickily through the window behind the young man's head.

'In the paper? There is something funny?'

There was something funny about the way he was pushing this, Rob thought. Funny in the head.

'No,' he said.

'Only you laughed.'

'It's a free country.'

It wasn't, but so what? It was just another of those things people said. Carol said. Like the condemned man's hearty breakfast. Didn't matter if it wasn't true. It was just a way of telling Tintin to fuck off without telling him to fuck off. Only the young man didn't seem to understand this, because he was picking up his empty glass and walking over. Which probably wasn't good. He held out his free hand.

'I'm Michael.'

Not good, okay, but probably not dangerous. Apart from the hair, he looked pretty normal. Tall. Skinny, under the shapeless sweatshirt. Good bones, Carol would have said. Something funny about the eyes, though.

Rob ignored the hand. 'The thing is, Michael, we don't do that round here.'

'Here?'

Rob shrugged, indicating the Prince. London. England. Anywhere, really. It was the same the whole world over, far as he knew. You didn't just walk over, stick out your paw and say hello. Why not? Well, because you might get stabbed, for starters.

No, that wasn't it. Look at him. He wasn't going to stab

anybody, was he? This guy Michael must see that. It was just . . . you didn't.

Michael said, 'What are you drinking?'

They didn't seem to move, the eyes. That was it.

'No, you're all right, thanks.'

Michael sat down, pointed at Rob's glass. 'I mean, what is that?'

Rob looked at his own glass. 'Bitter.'

'Bitter?'

'Best.'

Michael laughed. 'Why is it best?'

Rob shrugged. 'That's what they call it.'

'Is there a worst bitter?'

There must be, Rob thought. He'd had a few contenders in his time. He said, 'You're not from here, are you?'

'I am from Bergen. In Norway.'

So that was it. There wasn't an accent Rob could detect. But just that . . . flatness he'd noticed from the off. As if the words weren't quite alive, or real.

'You speak very good English.'

'Thank you. You also.'

What? Did the guy think he was some kind of foreigner, too? Was that why he'd come over?

'To the manner born, me.'

'Ha, ha. Very good. Because this pub is the Prince of Denmark, yes?'

'I'm sorry?'

'*Hamlet.* We read Shakespeare in school.'

'Right. Me too.' School was a long time ago, but yes, he had read *Hamlet*. And – the other one? – *Twelfth Night?*

'Of course, Fortinbras is Norwegian. Perhaps that's why.'

Rob knew he shouldn't, but he had to ask. 'Who's Fortinbras?'

Michael looked at him for a moment, perhaps trying to tell if he was joking.

'School was a long time ago,' Rob conceded.

'Go, bid the soldiers shoot.'

'What?'

Was that some kind of threat?

'The last words of the play, remember? Like, a salute. Fortinbras is the one who turns up and takes over Denmark when everybody else is dead.'

'Result.'

Michael grinned. 'Readiness is all. Hamlet's father killed Fortinbras' father, so perhaps it is only fair.'

Rob said, 'I think I'll have that pint after all.'

Go bid the soldiers shoot? He'd thought it was some kind of threat.

'I did not offer, but okay. Best bitter?' Michael spoke as if ordering a foreign delicacy he didn't quite trust. But also as if he knew it, and was mocking himself. The way Rob had once asked for *cheval?* in Belgium and Carol laughed. Try anything once. Mocking me, too, though, Rob thought. Michael, not Carol. Carol had just been laughing.

'And a short one with it.'

'A what?'

Finally, something the Norwegian know-all didn't know. 'A whisky.'

'A whisky and a beer?'

'Live dangerously. As they say.'

'Live every day as if it were your last?'

Christ, thought Rob. He'd almost forgotten.

'That's really not a good idea.'

Tomorrow was another day. Which was the fucking problem. Why he was where he was.

'No,' said Michael. 'I think not, too.'

It was still raining. At Rob's house, they hung their dripping overcoats in the hall. He showed Michael the spare room where he could dump his stuff and where, tonight, he could sleep. Tomorrow would be another day. He could take his pick then.

'The sofa folds out,' Rob said.

'It is from IKEA. My parents have this bed at home.'

'Right.'

What else was he supposed to say? Comparing notes on Swedish furniture wasn't exactly living dangerously.

'Bathroom's there. Sort yourself out, then I'll get some lunch together.'

First he had to take his pills. He wasn't usually so long in the Prince and now he was an hour overdue. Not that it mattered any more. Just habit, wasn't it? No, it wasn't. His blood pressure could drop through the floor while his mood shot through the ceiling. He couldn't afford to be wobbly.

Go bid the soldiers shoot.

Point and shoot.

Any fool.

Rob swallowed his lunchtime pills, finishing off one of the blue-backed blister packs. No problem. He'd picked up more that morning, along with everything else.

Downstairs in the hall, his coat hung next to Michael's, two small pools of water on the vinyl floor beneath them just about to merge. He remembered standing at the bar, crushing the chemist's bag into the left-hand pocket. It wasn't there. There was nothing there. Nothing in the right-hand pocket, either. Shit.

Michael? Could Michael have nicked them?

No.

Why not?

He didn't know why not. It just . . . it wasn't Michael.

Re-create the scene. The last known movements of all his drugs. At the bar, pills in left pocket, pint in right hand. Over to the table. He'd hung the coat over the back of his chair. That was it. Must have fallen out then. Must have. There was no point going back or calling Alistair. The pub had filled up by the time they left. Any drugs on the floor, they'd be long gone. Warfarin. Rennies. Diazepam. Didn't matter what.

He'd have to re-order. Surely they'd notice that? He'd have to explain, to phone the surgery. Which was pretty much impossible these days. Even if he went in, he wouldn't see the doctor. They'd leave a message; it would be a couple of days before he could collect replacements from the pharmacy.

He had his stockpile, though he didn't like dipping into it.

Another couple of days? He'd be all right. You couldn't live every day as if it were your last. That way you'd never start a book, or get the groceries in. Rob wasn't much of a reader. All his bills were paid.

Would Michael stay? He'd never planned on having

someone like Michael here. He'd always thought it would be Carol.

Point and shoot.

Any fool could do it.

Go bid the soldiers shoot.

He liked the sound of that. Someone to pick up the pieces.

He started making lunch.

Someone Like You

THIS MORNING A young defendant grabbed my note-book and waved it at the court. I don't know what he expected to find, or what reaction he anticipated. We were only three: myself, the usher, and the stenographer. There was no prosecutor. Given the circumstances, I have perforce adopted certain aspects of the continental method, although I have to say it goes against the grain.

Every day my fellow citizens parade before me for judgment.

Guilty.

Not guilty.

One year. Three. Six months.

Banishment.

Restitution.

Mine is not a real court, although I am – I was – a real judge. There is no wooden panelling, and only a scarred kitchen table for a bench; I wear no robes, no wig, and have no gavel to strike resoundingly as I bring order to my courtroom. (I never had. The persistence of gavels, as so much else in fiction, is a lie.) I have no courtroom.

The young man had apparently been a decorator. He

offered no evidence to justify the claim, however, no splash of paint on the plain wool three-piece suit he wore. He may perhaps have joined us on a Sunday.

He turned, waving my stolen notebook aloft, declaiming to the usher, to the stenographer, to the heath around us and – for all I know – to the crowd of rapt, or bored, or jeering witnesses that populated his deluded mind. He denied the legitimacy of my court, and – undeterred by the obvious paucity of its resources – denounced the "great organization" he somehow believed to stand behind his arrest, conjuring up a vast conspiracy of informers and policemen, detectives, gaolers and judges, along with our supposed retinues of servants and administrators. Finally, to my surprise – for pleading "not guilty" has always been a far cry from claiming innocence – he professed his conscience clear of any charge I might have been about to bring against him.

I did not rise, did not challenge his impertinence, but merely allowed him to leave. I will decide what charges he must face another day. Which may include the theft of my notebook.

On those rare days when my services are not required, when no one has committed adultery, born false witness or coveted his neighbour's ox, I read, I take a coffee, I play chess and sip a small glass of vile wine at the remains of the café in what must once have been an unattractive square; I stroll in the woods, the water meadows, exploring the boundaries of our demesne.

It does not take long.

There are no woods, of course, no water meadows. There may be a river, though: a loop of inky black water circumscribes our southern border without, apparently, flowing anywhere. Perhaps it is a lake?

Or I remain at home, in the bosom of my family.

I have no family.

There was a child, I recall, and must once have been a wife. *To have so soon 'scap'd world's and flesh's rage / And if no other misery, yet age.* The boy went rather earlier than Ben Jonson's, but rests, I trust, in the same soft peace. I can't say the same for his mother.

Justice is blind for a reason.

When I left court without my notebook, the afternoon was fair; the rain, when it fell, was light, the breeze soft. I had lately been pondering the validity of the appeal process. Justice is not justice if it does not admit the possibility of mistakes, but to hear appeals against oneself requires a certain – how shall I put it? –*flexibility* of mind. It is not a perfect system, but is perhaps better than the alternative.

Having completed a satisfactory stroll, I looked in at the café, hoping to encounter some opposition, but resigned to beating myself at chess if necessary.

As I entered, the clientele – crowd is really too strong a word – was not arrayed in conversational twos and threes, or huddled over solitary drinks, in the ordinary way, but had turned as one, like daisies in the sun, towards a figure standing at the counter on a low stool with his back towards them, one arm held dramatically aloft. Some species of mountebank, no doubt. Purveyors of indulgence and false consolation blow in from time to time to separate our citizens from what little money they possess; or, failing that, to extract a drink, a meal, a bed for the night. In the morning, they disappear again, leaving nothing but the vague disease that arises from a glimpse of indistinct, unrealized alternatives. There is harm in them, certainly, but unfortunately no crime.

This particular specimen was short and slight – hence the stool, I supposed – and draped in a ragged grey cloak that showed signs of having served as a blanket while its owner slept in a ditch. As I tried to catch the proprietor's eye – proprietor is undoubtedly the wrong word, too; his name is Peter – the mountebank turned to deliver the punch line, the denouement, the deal-closing pitch of his routine and I realized, to my surprise, that she was a woman, and that I knew her.

'Lina?'

She hesitated no more than a fraction of a second before completing her turn, flinging out the arm she'd held aloft to point unerringly at a figure in the middle of the café – the mayor, accompanied by two or three of his principal functionaries, all with glasses frozen half way to their mouths. *'Monsieur le maire . . .'* she cried: *'J'accuse!'*

There was a moment's silence before the mayor, first, then his functionaries, and finally everyone in the café clapped and roared with laughter, wiped tears from their eyes and repeated to each other, *J'accuse, j'accuse.* Did you hear that? They shook their heads. *J'accuse!*

Lina hopped down from the stool and picked her way past customers who slapped her on the back, raised their glasses and offered to buy her drinks, until she reached the mayor's table. He stood and bowed – bowed! – wiped his beard with the back of his hand and gestured that she should take a seat. At that moment, the rain returned, falling gently between the remaining roof beams, darkening the tabletops, diluting the sour wine. No one paid it any heed.

I turned back to Peter and managed finally to order. I took my drink and the chess set to an empty table in the corner. Lina would have to come to me, if she had anything to say.

She did, although for the moment she was happy saying it to the mayor, who seemed uncharacteristically willing to listen; who, indeed, hung on every word. In time, though, she left him, tucking a heavy purse out of sight beneath her cloak, and picked her way between the increasingly damp tables to where I sat, studying the board in front of me. She slid a black knight out from behind its pawns to threaten the white king.

'Check.'

I shook my head. It was a clumsy, or possibly deliberate, mistake. 'Mate in three,' I said.

'I should be so lucky.'

I raised my eyes. She had lost weight, and there were lines around her eyes. Otherwise, I told myself, she had not changed.

I said, 'You left.'

'You sent me away.'

I let that pass. It was true, after all.

I gestured to Peter who, correctly interpreting my signal, brought over a bottle of his least filthy vintage, and a second glass.

She pulled up a chair and accepted a drink. 'You owe me that, at least,' she said.

I owed her nothing.

She sipped her wine. 'Let me tell you something in return.'

'As long as it isn't a story.'

She said, 'Once upon a time,' and grinned.

'Oh, please.'

'It's what I do now, Max.'

In truth she had always been a storyteller. A telltale. One of those who would run to the adults, whose hand would shoot up when the teacher entered a rowdy classroom demanding to know exactly what was going on. I hadn't known her when she was at school.

'Once upon a time there was a judge who wasn't a real judge . . .'

'It's not about me, then?'

'I told you, it's a story. It's not about you.'

I sat back, sipped my wine and closed my eyes. I might as well allow her to continue. The sooner she started, the sooner she would finish.

'He wasn't a real judge, but he'd been a solicitor's clerk before he was arrested. In the camp, that was all it took. Prisoners caught stealing from each other would, if they were lucky, be dragged before him to decide how long they'd spend in isolation, or the severity of their beatings.

'In prison you need a specialism to survive: trade, violence, a craft. The judge's only specialism was impartiality. He did not care for his fellow prisoners, so his judgments were fair. He spotted malicious prosecutions motivated by advantage or revenge. His fees were reasonable.

'In time, his reputation grew. The authorities began to value his expertise. They gave him the power to sentence prisoners to death, or to additional work – which generally meant the same thing. Soon after that, he was accused of collaboration. It troubled him deeply. He thought about it long and hard, pacing the boundaries of the prison, worrying late into the night.

'It wasn't the morality that bothered him. If collaboration could keep him alive, he'd welcome it. But collaboration might undermine his specialism, his reputation for impartiality. It might threaten his ability to survive.

'What was he to do?

'One day . . .'

I sighed and opened my eyes. 'Here we go.'

Lina ignored me. 'One day, after morning roll call, he was pulled from the line and marched to the governor's office. The governor did not look up as he dismissed the guard. The judge stood to attention while the governor finished reading a memorandum. There were two empty chairs in front of the governor's desk, but he was not invited to sit.

'After a while the governor laid the memorandum aside. Without looking up, he said: "How are you this morning?"

'The judge had to consider this. It was not a question one asked a prisoner. Eventually he said, "I am content."

'The governor looked up, then. "Content?"

'The judge nodded but said nothing more.

'Then the governor said, "There is a female prisoner here, Irene G – you may have heard of her?"

'He had.

'"This woman has presented certain . . . problems."

'The judge had not met Irene, but he knew her story. She'd arrived the previous November, when the sky was white with snow and the fields already frozen. She'd been denounced by her own husband, and it was said that, in the eight days it took the train to cross the mountains and the plain, she had not once ceased to plan what she would do to him when she was released – or, better still, escaped. When the other prisoners told her there was no escape, and no release, she did not believe them. "How could you live like that," she said, "without hope of change?" "Certainly, there is change," they said. "In the spring it is not so cold; in the summer we work longer hours, but there is more food; in winter we are given an extra shirt."

'She was horrified. Not by the prison itself, which was no worse than she'd expected, but by her fellow prisoners' refusal to challenge its conditions. She tried to organize them into committees – to plan escapes, to lobby the governor for more blankets, to be allowed to drink their soup while it was still hot. It all came to nothing.

'The judge assumed these were not the problems the governor meant. There had been other agitators – not many, it was true, but a handful. He'd had no trouble hanging them.

'The governor said, "She began a hunger strike."

'He'd heard that, too. No one joined in. The other prisoners were not sympathetic: they were outraged. There had been fights for the food she refused. Still, it could not last long.

'"Two prisoners, a man and a woman," the governor continued, "were so incensed, they tried to kill her. They worked in the canteen and had stolen blunt knives. They were trying to slit open her mouth so they could force food into her when another prisoner – a trustee who had, in fact, been ordered to force feed her himself – intervened. In their rage, the prisoners turned on him instead. They forced him to the ground. The woman stabbed at his chest and the man was about to slash his throat when Irene G told them to stop. She said she would eat if only they would stop."

'The governor paused. He had been fiddling with something on his desk, the lid of an inkwell, perhaps, spinning it like a top. Now he reached out and slapped it still. "Tell me: what would you have done?"

'The judge said, "If I were Irene G?"

'"If you were one of the other prisoners. Would you have stopped?"

'He had no idea. "I would not have been in that situation."

'"But if you were? Put yourself in their shoes."

'He shook his head. He could not be a judge if he put himself in other people's shoes. And if he were not a judge, he would not survive.

'He said, "I can't."'

Lina stopped. She drained her glass and reached for the bottle. I became aware that I was not her only auditor, although she had not raised her voice. Conversations around the café had gradually died; customers had edged closer in their chairs. Only the mayor's table remained aloof, the functionaries' voices loud and their smiles fixed as they demonstrated their loyalty.

Lina said, 'So – what would you have done?'

'You said this wasn't about me.'

'It's about someone *like* you. Who does what you do.'

'Oh, I thought you meant: would I have stabbed the trustee?'

Lina laughed and drank more wine. 'Liar.'

The truth was: I had no idea.

The truth was: I couldn't help seeing it through the eyes of Lina's judge.

I said, 'It wouldn't work like that.'

'It's my story,' she said. 'It works the way I say it works. That's the beauty of stories.'

I said, 'I'd try the case.'

'Of course.' She waited. 'Which case?'

'Ah. Did the trustee die?'

'Let's assume he did.'

'And what did your judge do?'

She took a breath and seemed, for a moment, to be debating with herself. Impatient mutterings arose from the tables around us. One man stood up noisily to buy another drink.

Eventually she said, 'The judge agreed to try the case.'

'And?'

'And the governor nodded slowly in response. "Naturally," he said. "What will your verdict be?"

'The judge said he would question those involved and examine the facts.

'"I have given you the facts."

'The judge demurred, but the governor interrupted him. "There can be no doubt in this case."

'"Then why ask me to try it?"

'"There must be a trial. But in a matter as delicate as this, I must know what you will conclude before I can allow it to proceed."

'"That's not how trials work."

'"This is a prison camp. Everything here works the way I say it works. That's the beauty of it."

'The judge did not reply.

'The governor said, "Is that your final answer?"'

Lina did not stay long. Like all those of her type, she extracted what she could, then left.

The following day, the decorator – if that is what he was – returned to court. He began by handing me back my notebook.

'There's nothing in it,' he said. 'What do you do all day?'

I dismissed the charges against him.

I looked out across the heath to where the river stood still, silent and black.

Out of habit, I said: 'You're free to go.'

The Good Neighbour
[REDACTED]

Subject	██████ ██████
Interviewers	██████ ██████
	██████
Date	11/11/████
Time	14:30

OKAY, WHAT CAN I tell you? I wouldn't say I know him well. I don't think anybody up here does, but I've probably seen more of him than most. Don't get me wrong. I've been a widow long enough to know I want to stay that way. It's just, there's only his place and mine on this road, you see? I try to be a good neighbour. You have to, up here, don't you? Anyway, the place was empty for a while after the ████s both died in the first wave. ███ moved in, must be – what? – four, five years ago, I suppose. It's the end of the road up there, so he comes past my house every time he goes down to the village or back. The ████s used to stop for a chat if I was at home, in the garden, say, which

I am a lot. ▮▮ isn't like that, but he'll say hello, sometimes, talk about the weather. You know. Or I'll see him in
the pub.

Not often – me, I'm behind the bar most nights; when it's
open – and he always has a book with him. Doesn't sit
at the bar with the other lads who come in alone. Or by
the stove, even when it's brass monkeys. He'll go over
to a table in the corner. He'll open his book and wait for
me to bring him a pint. He's not looking for company, is
what I'm saying; but if I speak to him, he'll be friendly
enough.

He told me he'd retired. I said he didn't look old enough.
That wasn't just pub talk. He really didn't look that old. He
said that's what his boss said, too. Also, that he couldn't
leave, there was a crisis. But he said there's always a crisis,
if it wasn't one thing it'd be another. I knew what he meant.
There's always something, isn't there? I mean, if it wasn't
the virus, it'd be, I don't know, the climate change. Or that
▮▮▮▮▮▮. What do they call it? Where the ▮▮▮▮▮ or
whoever wreck computers? Or there'd be another famine
somewhere, or a war.

Sorry. Right. I asked him what he did, before, and he said he
was a civil servant. You'll know that, anyway. He said he'd
had enough. Also that he *had* enough – meaning money,
his pension. That's the thing about the civil service, isn't
it? Always used to be, anyway. He said it wasn't much –
which depends, doesn't it? On what you're used to. He said
anyway there wasn't much to spend it on up here. I thought:

you wait till the windows on that house need re-painting, or the roof starts to leak. It won't be long, either, the weather we get here. You've been down to the shore? Beautiful, all right, but vicious cold, sometimes. You're standing on the rocks, looking out across the loch, and there's that island? Not a trace of life since the ██████ ██████ mob used it to test some ██████ weapon, during the last war? It wasn't the last war, of course, but you know what I mean. Anyway, beyond that, there's nothing from here to the North Pole. Not even ice, these days. And the wind . . . Anyway, he used to be a civil servant. ██████ ████, I think he said, but he wouldn't say much more. All secret, I suppose. Hush-hush. I don't need to tell you that. Anyway, the impression I got, he was just fed up with it, whatever it was he did.

No, not wrong. Just said he had nothing to offer. His wife died in the third wave, you know. But it wasn't that. He was just fed up with pretending he had any answers, he said, and waiting to be found out. That's what he said. You remember how we used to count the waves? Until we realized there wasn't any point?

No. Hadn't even been here on holiday. That's what most of them do, you know. Come up for a week in early May, before the midges really get going. They come back a year or two later, find the place still here, still lovely. Come back once more, they think they can retire here. Don't know that January feels like a whole year in itself. ████'s not like that, though. He barely seems to notice. Which takes some doing when it's dark at three in the afternoon, I can tell you, or light till midnight. He'll plod down to the shop, whatever, plod up again, stop in for a coffee sometimes, call me over for a drink during lockdowns once or twice, down to the pub a couple of times a month, I'd say, when it's open.

Me? No. Been here forty years, though. Came for a summer job, fell in love. You know how it is. Started behind the bar at the hotel, ended up running the place. When there was a hotel. Now I'm back behind a bar. The circle of life. It keeps me busy. Are you sure you want all this?

So, okay. I was there, as it happens, when ████ turned up. You know what they say about bad pennies? I'm only joking. Because that was her name. I didn't even know he had a daughter. ██ girl, ██ ██ hair. I say girl, she must have been forty, but quite a looker, really. Sorry. Anyway, we were in his house for once. The sitting room is tiny, but it has this huge picture window, and we were standing there watching the sunset light up the clouds from underneath, the way it does, and there's someone trudging up the road from the village. She's half a mile away, and the light's getting dim. ██ hands me his binoculars and asks: Is it a woman? Has she got ██ hair? Well, I have to adjust the eyepieces – he really must have terrible sight – and then I can see her, clear as day, bag slung across her shoulders, bumping on her hip. Not the sort of bag that makes any sense round here. But yes, she's a woman and her hair's the colour of a ████ ████, if you've ever seen one of those. Anyway. That's ████, he said. We watched her stop at the cattle grid and turn to look back the way she'd come, out to sea. He said he'd done that, too, the first time. I said I should be getting off home, leave them to it, but he asked me to stay. He said he'd introduce me, but now I think of it, he sounded nervous. I asked when he'd last seen his daughter, and he said it was before he moved up here. He'd called a couple of times, he said; she emailed him. They were Facebook friends, but neither of them ever posted anything. When she got up to the house, he opened the door and held his arms out wide for a hug, but she didn't move. Just stood there in this big padded coat and city shoes. She said she had to keep her distance, even here. The regulations, you know. She shouldn't be here, she said, much less touch him. Which might all be true, I remember thinking, but was utterly beside the point. She didn't want a hug.

Call it a mother's intuition. I could see her as a child, when her daddy threw his arms around her. She'd have stood stock still, or sat on his lap, not complaining, not moving, but her arms at her sides. It would have been like cuddling a golf bag. I know that feeling. Still, he'd have persisted, I thought. But he stepped back now, letting her come in without getting too close. He introduced me, explained I lived in the house she'd just walked by. She drops her bag like a soldier dumping kit in a new barracks. Settling in, but not anywhere she'd ever think of as home. He offered tea. She looks at her watch, then out the window at the dying light and asks if he hasn't anything stronger. He said he had whisky, because it keeps well. He said he doesn't often drink these days. The side effects of his medication are scary enough to make him take the alcohol warnings seriously, he said, looking at me, like I'm supposed to back him up. Or at least not rat him out. He pours us a small glass each and raises his. So, he says. So, she says, sipping hers, not giving anything away. *Slàinte mhath*, he says, the way I taught him. To what do I owe the pleasure? She shakes her head. Don't do that, Dad. Do what? he says. She sips her whisky again, then turns to the window, looking out over the bay. She says, Can I stay? He laughs and says: You can hardly head back tonight, sweetheart. (He called her sweetheart.) There's no bus till Monday, for starters. But she meant could she *stay*? Even I could see that.

And then he sat down, knees cracking like logs on a fire. Sat where he always sits, in the armchair with the wooden arms and a view of the sea. There's only one other chair in that little room, so it's a bit awkward, ▮▮▮ and me both standing there, but he didn't seem to notice. He told her to sit down. I said I really should be going, but he took no notice. Finally, with a glance at me like some sort of apology, she sits down, and he says: Perhaps you should tell me why you're here? She says, Does there have to be a reason? and he says: There's always something. She takes a sip of whisky and says if she told him she'd killed someone, would he believe her?

Pretty much. She said: *If I said I'd killed someone, would you believe me?* It's not the sort of thing you could forget.

Well, he said no. And she said: That's why I'm here. Then

after a while, he said: Have you? And she laughed, and said:
Oh, probably. Haven't we all by now?

I guess. I've been over and over it in my mind, if that's what
you mean.

After that? After that I said I really must be going, I had to
get my supper on. He tried to get me to stay, offered to cook
for us all, which wasn't something he'd ever done before.
We didn't have that kind of relationship. I mean, a biscuit
with a cup of tea, maybe, but not cooking. Not a meal. It
was as though he was scared to let me leave. Then ████
said she wasn't hungry, she was tired. It had been a long
journey, and she'd like to go to bed; they could talk in the
morning. He showed her up to his spare room, then came
down and asked if I'd have another drink. I said I really
shouldn't, but he poured it anyway.

I asked about her, why he'd never mentioned her before.
He said they weren't close. I said, But you'd like to be? He
just sort of shrugged. Said she was a civil servant, too. A
chip off the old block, I said; and he said: something like
that. I was thinking: too alike to get on well, perhaps. You
know how it can be. More often with fathers and sons, I'd
have thought. That's the way it was with my two, anyway.
Always fighting over nothing. We never had a girl, more's
the pity. Anyway, she was in the ████████ of ████, he
said, and doing really well. Better than he had. She'd be
Perm Sec one day, he said: Permanent Secretary, you know.
I made some joke about office temps that probably wasn't
funny, just trying to lighten the mood. He was proud of her,

but he'd had a face on him like Bela Lugosi ever since she arrived.

That's what he said. Of course, now we know that wasn't going to happen, don't we? But we didn't then. I don't think he did. I might be wrong, but I don't think she could have told him.

I didn't see them the next day. It was a Sunday. I never see him on a Sunday. I go to church; I stop by ████'s grave; I go home. ████ does whatever the godless do on a Sunday, but at least he does it indoors, as far as I know.

So, Monday I'm out sweeping up leaves, it must have been about eleven o'clock when ████ goes by, empty shopping bag in one hand, walking stick in the other, like nothing's changed. When obviously everything's changed. I call out and he comes over. I ask how ████ is and he says she's gone. I ask how come – the bus doesn't even leave till two o'clock – and he says she left yesterday.

Exactly. Sunday. That's what I said. She just has, he says. I invite him in and it looks like he's going to refuse, but then he doesn't. He follows me indoors and sits down while I put the kettle on. He says that in the night he thought he heard her crying. He got out of bed and tiptoed down the hall, avoiding the creakiest floorboards. Even so, she heard him. I'm all right, she called out. Go back to bed. When she was a girl, he said, it had been the same. She could be sobbing, tears running down her face, and she would tell him she was fine. Six, seven years old. She'd tell him to go back to bed, back to his desk, back to whatever he had been doing without her. ▮▮▮▮ – that was his wife – sometimes got a bit more out of her, he said, but nothing you wouldn't expect. Friends falling out, pets dying, impossible homework, boys. Then, from about fourteen or fifteen: nothing.

No, and I didn't ask. He said she was forty now, her birthday a couple of months back. Facebook reminded him, but it was already too late. He couldn't just send a message on the day, could he? So he sent nothing at all. Why couldn't they warn you in advance? That's what he said. I don't use it myself. I asked was he okay, though it was pretty obvious he wasn't. In the morning, he said, Sunday morning, she was up first. He could hear her in the kitchen making breakfast. He went down and she looked full of beans, bustling about, scrambling eggs, buttering toast. She said she hoped he didn't mind. Of course he didn't. He said she must have had a good night's sleep and she said yes. She said everything looked much clearer now.

That's what I said, but he wasn't really listening. Just talking. Almost like I wasn't there. They ate breakfast and he asked how long she had off work. She laughed, and he said it reminded him of ▮▮▮▮, then. She said she wasn't going back. He said of course she was. But it turns out she'd resigned, couldn't go back if she wanted to. He stopped talking. I asked was he all right, again, and this time he said: she told me what she'd done. I asked what that was, and he just said: what I should have done.

His exact words, yes. *She did what I should have done.*

I asked, but he just said he hadn't dared. He'd come up here instead, but now she was here as well. I asked if he meant he should have resigned earlier, not waited for his pension, and he said yes, but not that. That wasn't what he was talking about. Then he started talking about that █████ scandal, a year ago, the one with all the birth defects and it turned out the company had got the order early, when we were all in a panic, before they'd finished all the tests, and only then because the CEO was somebody's brother-in-law. Just before the election. I forget the details, I said, to keep him talking. Was it the one with the whistleblower? Where the journalist was on trial because he wouldn't say who it was? He just looked at me for a while, shook his head. He wasn't really there, in my kitchen. He was off somewhere, Parliament, maybe, or Whitehall, anyway. The ████████ ████████, wherever that is.

He said she'd told him she was going for a walk. He offered to go too, show her the village, not that there's much to it, but she said she meant a proper walk. Up in the hills. She had a map and everything and could she make herself a packed lunch? He said was she sure she wanted to go alone, and where exactly did she have in mind and don't forget it would be dark by four o'clock. And that's the last he saw of her. She wasn't back by four, he said. When she wasn't back at six, he knew something must be wrong. I asked if he called the mountain rescue number and he said no and when I asked why not he said he'd gone to take his pills and there was a full packet missing – four weeks' worth – and her clothes were all there and her city shoes and her bag but the whisky was gone too, and when I said you have to call the police, you must, he wouldn't, so I did, and here you are.

Yes, no, I know you're not police, as such. I try to help, that's all.

Interview terminated at 14:58

Smoker Required

MY FATHER, GORDON *Hanbury, was ill for a long time. When he died, six years ago now, at the age of fifty-eight, his affairs were very much in order. Apart from his books – which were immaculately arranged – and his smoking paraphernalia, he owned very few possessions, and none of any value. He had no debts, owned his flat outright, and kept meticulous records of his savings, pension and insurance policies. His will was clear: my mother and I were to share his estate equally. Probate would be straightforward. None of this – except, perhaps, the balance on the savings account he had opened only months earlier – came as any surprise to those who knew him.*

Among all the order, it was easy to overlook the occasional eccentricities: the glass-topped coffee table with no glass top; the pyramid of rare, empty cigarette packets on the mantelpiece; the pages of the small black notebook left on the desk overlooking the cemetery in which, among all the to-do lists, meeting notes and expenses to be reclaimed, he had written the account of his last summer, which is presented here. I certainly overlooked the latter at the time, and only recently discovered it while clearing out my apartment in preparation for a return to London.

The story – it would be stretching a point to call it memoir, let alone confession – clearly displays my father's weakness for self-aggrandizing fantasy: the shadowy PIs with their concealed "gats"; the Bank of England job, with its long, alcoholic lunches at the French Embassy; the literary pretension; the international conspiracy of smokers. For all that, it portrays a truth about my father – as a man, a husband and, for what it's worth, a father – that deserves to be known.

My father was not, on the whole, a happy man, and he did not make those around him happy. If tobacco brought him peace, if it contributed towards his early death, that was a consolation he was able to purchase far too cheaply.

◊

Strolling through Knightsbridge on a cool overcast Saturday afternoon earlier this summer, I spotted a tiny handwritten advertisement in a newsagent's window: *Smoker required (tobacco). Generous rates. Enquire within.* It was twelve years to the day since the introduction of the smoking ban, an anniversary that few people, I imagine, would recall, much less mark in any way; but I am very much a smoker.

The City, not Knightsbridge, is my natural habitat. For reasons I no longer recall, however, I had visited the Victoria & Albert Museum for the first time in decades – quite possibly for the first time since being frog-marched around the place, one of a platoon of doubtless intolerable schoolchildren, half a century ago – after which, with little else to occupy my time, I decided to walk the mile or so to Victoria Station, and my train home. It was as I picked my way through the smaller streets between Harrods and

Sloane Square that I came across the newsagent's window with its brief but intriguing advertisement. A smoker was required, and I was a smoker in a world where, these days, we are very much not required at all.

I enquired within.

The man behind the counter was slight, with dark eyes and jet-black hair. Feeling the need to establish my goodwill before interrogating him about the notice in his window, I requested twenty Rothmans. When he handed me my change, I was reminded that, in the days when I first seriously attempted to give up smoking, a packet of twenty cigarettes cost just £1. Each abstinent evening, I would place a pound coin in a glass jar until, after a month, I had accumulated sufficient cash to visit the tobacconist in the Burlington Arcade that sold the sort of Turkish and Russian cigarettes I could never normally afford. In those days Rothmans came with the name printed in white on a blue shield: the crest, the words 'King Size' and the banner – 'By Special Appointment' – were all embossed in gold. These days, the packet carries photographs of diseased organs.

It had been a woman who placed the advertisement, apparently.

'Did she leave a contact number? An address?'

Apparently not.

'She said, if anyone asks, I should say to contact Sarah Slother.'

'But how?'

The man shrugged.

Could he tell me anything more? Had she been young? Old? Tall? Short? Fat? Thin?

He shrugged again. Apparently she had been none of these.

She had red hair, though, he remembered that. Red like the sky when the sun sets over the ocean, he said.

The man was a poet, I thought, not kindly.

At home, my desk occupies a bay window in the living room of my first floor flat, overlooking the southern boundary wall of a large Victorian cemetery. Waiting for my computer to come to life, I reflected that the Internet must have changed so many lives, not least those of Private Investigators. I googled Sarah Slother and in less than a second discovered why, despite being certain I knew no one of that name, it had nonetheless tugged at the corners of my memory all the way home.

It had been more than thirty years since, as a student of modern European literature, I read Thomas Bernhard's *Concrete*. I nonetheless found my copy without difficulty (one of the benefits of shelving one's books logically, of which I never could convince my wife, Elaine). About a third of the way through the novel our narrator Rudolph visits a near neighbour – a former cavalry officer in the First World War, an old man who is not named but lives in a damp, decaying, four-hundred-year-old pile, and calls himself a baron. He tells Rudolph that he has decided to leave everything not to his daughter, nor to the church or state, but to a name and address picked at random from a London telephone directory: Sarah Slother, 128 Knightsbridge. He chuckles at his own deviousness. Critics, I now recalled, had been struck by this passage. Why would an Austrian cavalry officer, still proud of the medal he received from the emperor, choose to leave his fortune to someone – anyone – in London? Why had Bernhard chosen this name, which, some thought, did not sound convincingly English? And why this address? Knightsbridge is a street, as well as a neighbourhood, so the address was not a mistake, as such; it nonetheless struck them as implausible. Knightsbridge is a wealthy area: how much difference would this surprise inheritance make to the already well-to-do occupant of number 128? In short, it was a jarring moment; one that, for good or ill – opinions differed – pulls the reader momentarily out of the narrator's claustrophobic solipsism. It had seemed to me, however, that the debate missed the real reason for the old man's cruel pleasure: he has no fortune; the crumbling mansion is a burden, a punishment, not a blessing. Such, at any rate, was the thesis of my hastily-constructed undergraduate essay, written through the night with nothing but instant coffee and Pro-Plus to sustain me.

Bernhard wrote *Concrete* in 1982. If Sarah Slother existed, she would by now be in her late fifties at the very least, and likely much, much older. Old enough that the newsagent might have remarked upon it? Even if she were fictional, however, the address was not. Knightsbridge certainly existed, and it would be easy enough, I thought then, to find number 128. In the book, the old man says he does not care who Sarah Slother is: he will leave everything he has to the address, whoever or whatever is inside. The building was the thing. The woman who left the advertisement might not be Sarah Slother; but her message, to those who could decode it, was that she could be found at 128 Knightsbridge. Evidently, it was not merely a smoker she required, but a reader, too; I could only conclude that in me she had found her man.

I typed the address into the search bar. Google Maps dropped a red pin just north of Knightsbridge, in a narrow gap between two buildings. I switched to Street View: a six-storey, balconied red brick mansion block. Most of the ground floor was occupied by an upmarket beauty parlour clearly identified as number 122. To the left was a glass and mahogany door discretely numbered 124, most likely the entrance to the flats above. Beyond that, where the map indicated a gap, I could see the blank brick wall of the Hyde Park barracks. There was no gap, no passage-way. Could numbers 126 and 128 have been swallowed by the barracks? It was possible, I thought. Google gave the barracks' address – confusingly – as 20A Knightsbridge. It also told me that the building had been opened in 1970: long before Bernhard wrote *Concrete*. I searched for number 128 once more, then 126 and 130. Again and again, Google landed pins in the passageway that did not exist. But it was then that I noticed an even narrower passage, marked on the map as a single blue line, to the right – the east – of the beauty parlour. Park Close. It was too narrow for Street View to penetrate. Although the pins suggested otherwise, perhaps the entrances to numbers 126-130 were in reality tucked away in there?

The following day – Sunday – my daughter paid one of her occasional visits to London. Having spent the previous evening with her mother, she summoned me to lunch at a restaurant in Clapham that specialized in fabricating elaborate mousses from the body parts of pigs that other chefs eschewed. Elizabeth was well; her mother had apparently never been better since adopting the Alexander technique. I didn't enquire. By the time lunch was over and I had dispatched Elizabeth and her impossibly tiny suitcase back towards Heathrow, I'd drunk too much and peered too long into the abyss to contemplate travelling up to Knightsbridge in search of Sarah Slother.

On Monday, however, I invented a lunch appointment at the French Embassy and left the City heading west, emerging from the underground at Hyde Park Corner. After lighting a cigarette, I cut through to South Carriage Drive where the traffic is lighter. It is one of the unfortunate side effects of the smoking ban that it so often forces one to smoke in the street, something I rarely did before 2007. I passed the embassy, which quite sensibly turns its back on Knightsbridge to face the park. Already, through the windows, I could see diplomats and civil servants at tables laid with thick white linen and heavy silver.

Park Close was cool, a narrow canyon as impenetrable to the summer sun as it had been to Google's cameras. Behind the beauty parlour I found a number 6 – presumably 6 Park Close – beyond which there was a further doorway, adorned with a double rank of bell buttons. Clearly, I thought, another entrance to the flats above, like that on the main road; just like that door, it was numbered 124. Beyond, were two properties: an Italian restaurant and a "luxury gents barber" which, logically, might have been numbers 126 and 128 respectively, but might just as logically have been numbers 5 and 4 – or even 4 and 2 – Park Close. Pity the poor postman in these parts, I thought. I took out my phone and pretended to make a call while photographing the restaurant and the barbershop. The flats

above appeared to be accessed by a final doorway, in the
fanlight over which was etched, in letters a foot high: *ONE*.

So there it was. Or rather, wasn't.

I retreated to a pub back on the main road, where I
ordered a pint of bitter and a salt beef burger, which at
least had the benefit of novelty, but which cost me rather
more than twenty pounds. I took my drink to a small
table, where, with my back against the wall, I had a good
view of the front half of the bar, and waited for my lunch.
Could the barbershop really be the home of Sarah Slother?
Perhaps I should have requested a haircut, and pumped the
proprietor? That's what a real PI – Sam Spade, perhaps
– would have done. I looked again at the photos on my
phone. There was no number on the Italian restaurant. But
the barber's door had been wedged open, and I realized
that I had not scrutinized it closely enough. I zoomed in,
and there, clearly visible despite the acute angle at which
the door stood open, was a brass number: 2. So that was
that. What had I learned? Only that there *was* no 128
Knightsbridge. Google Maps will tell you otherwise, but
Google Maps is lying. Thomas Bernhard never heard of
Google – he died in 1986 – but still, I thought, he'd had
the last laugh. Except it wasn't Bernhard, was it, who had
placed the advert in the newsagent's window? Someone
else was laughing, too.

When my lunch arrived, it turned out not to be a burger
made of salt beef, but two ordinary burger patties between
which hunks of salt beef had been sandwiched. A few years
earlier I had caught the beady eye of the medical profes-
sion when a routine check-up revealed catastrophic levels
of cholesterol in my blood. Ah well, I'd told Elizabeth,

blowing smoke towards the ceiling from the corner of my mouth, a heart attack would probably be a better way to go than lung cancer.

A woman asked if everything was all right. She meant my lunch, and I assured her that it was.

Once I had eaten, I decided to stroll down to Harrods – my fictitious engagement at the French Embassy would undoubtedly have lasted several hours and involved at least two bottles of wine – wondering idly if I might find a replacement coffee table for my flat – the current one having been somewhat *hors de combat* since I moved in – but soon realized my mistake. They used to say one could buy anything at Harrods. Now it is five floors of nothing anyone would want. Russian oligarch chic. Was ever anything so vulgar?

As I re-emerged onto the Brompton Road and paused to light a cigarette, a young man begged my pardon and thrust a piece of paper towards me. 'Please,' he said. I took the paper, if only to be rid of him, stuffed it into my jacket pocket, and began to walk.

'Read it,' he called after me. 'It relates to your search.'

I waited as long as I could bear – as long as it took to finish my cigarette – before pulling out the paper to read: *Sarah.slother82@gmail.com*. Nothing else.

Now what?

I emailed her then and there, from the street, something that, in normal circumstances, I would never do. Before I could find a café to await a reply, it arrived. I was to make my way to the Serpentine. Starting at the Lido at 3.00 p.m., I read – it was then 2.35 – I should circumnavigate the lake clockwise, proceeding at a moderate pace but without stopping, or looking back. It should take around an hour, the email said, in the course of which I was to smoke at least three cigarettes. It was addressed *Dear Mr Hanbury* and signed, *Yours sincerely, Sarah Slother.*

Why not? I thought. French economists – not least fictional French economists – can be verbose, as well as bibulous; no one would be surprised if I did not return to the Bank at all that afternoon.

There were no heavies waiting for me at the Lido – or if there were, they remained discretely out of sight, their suits doubtless tailored to disguise the gats holstered underneath their armpits. On a convenient bench I waited, smoking and enjoying the sunshine in the trees, while the hands on my watch crept up on three o'clock. Then – no one having approached, or sat beside me, or left a folded newspaper for me on the bench – I rose, lit a fresh cigarette, and sauntered off towards the bridge.

An hour and three cigarettes later – I had regulated my pace effectively – I found myself back at the Lido, none the wiser. At one point, turning a corner in the Italian Gardens, and stepping aside to avoid a tall roller skater with headphones like coconut halves clamped about her ears, I thought I caught a glimpse of red hair some twenty feet behind me. I continued towards the Sackler Gallery without looking back again. Whatever Sarah Slother required a smoker for, the role was clearly to be undertaken on her terms or not at all.

I was not mistaken. That evening, I received a second email, to which was attached an employment contract: I was invited to add my name and address, and to confirm

my right to work in the United Kingdom. My proba-
tionary trial had been successful, I was informed: I was
already owed £100. All that was required was for me to
sign and return the completed contract, and to provide
my bank details. The money would then be transferred
to my account, and further engagements would follow,
for which I would be paid at the standard rate of £100
per hour.

I poured myself a glass of wine and beat egg yolks for
a carbonara. It made a change from Nigerian princes, I
supposed. I fried pancetta and grated parmesan. It had
been well pitched. £100 an hour was very good money by
most people's standards, without appearing preposterous.
Not a sum that would change your life, or sound too good
to be true.

Surely it was not true?

And yet, I thought, judging that I had time for one
more cigarette before the pasta reached al dente, had not
the whole set-up been a little elaborate for a petty fraud?
You could hardly hope to recruit many – what was the
conman's word? – many *marks* by advertising for smokers
in a Knightsbridge newsagent. Not these days. There could,
I supposed, be similar advertisements in shops across the
city that I had simply never noticed, but it would be ridic-
ulously labour intensive to observe everyone who arrived
in search of the non-existent address. Besides, how many
people would make the connection? The reason those
emails from Nigerian princes are so wretchedly written, I
had once heard at a conference on fraud prevention, is not
because the fraudsters are themselves illiterate, but because
it filters out those readers smart enough to notice, thereby

increasing the subsequent hit rate. Here, however, we had an approach that could only attract the attention of readers familiar with one of the lesser-known works of a twentieth-century Austrian modernist whose sales in this country had, with all due respect, been minuscule.

What were the odds?

Bizarre as it seemed, I was almost certain that what "Sarah Slother" wanted was not to steal my identity or the contents of my bank account, but for me to walk, in public, smoking.

Why she might want me to do so remained a mystery, but she was apparently prepared to pay for the privilege. Perhaps, like me, she was one of nature's smokers? Perhaps, having been instructed not to smoke on medical grounds, she nonetheless found herself missing the scent of tobacco. Perhaps, having unexpectedly inherited the small fortune of an Austrian baron, she had decided to spend it on indulging the private but essentially harmless luxury of employing someone – employing *me* – to walk, and smoke, so that she could follow close behind, reminding herself of the pleasures of the leaf.

The pasta was almost done. I took the cheesecake I had bought at Zobler's out of the fridge. It would taste better if it were not too chilled.

Of course, there was no Austrian baron; I knew that. It was a novel. Besides, even if he had been real, if there had been an old man who chose to leave his fortune to a random English woman – so much of Bernhard's fiction was based, after all, on real events – he would have been approaching eighty-five in 1982 and would have died decades ago. Why would Sarah – even if she existed – be advertising now?

I should proceed with caution.

I ate the pasta but returned the cheesecake to the fridge. Perhaps, after tagliatelle carbonara, it would be a little too much, even for me? I undressed, brushed my teeth and flushed my daily statin tablet down the toilet.

The following day, from the privacy of my office, I opened a new online deposit account, transferring just £1. I worked a little late, catching up on emails and making amends for the previous day. Once the floor was quiet enough, I printed off the contract, completed my personal details, signed, scanned and returned a copy to Sarah. Slother82@gmail.com, along with the details of my new account. I left just before eight-thirty. By the time I arrived home I had already received a text from the bank confirming the deposit of £100, and another email, welcoming me to Sarah Slother's employment and instructing me to report to the Serpentine Lido at 3.00 p.m. the day after tomorrow (i.e. Thursday) whence I should proceed as before, albeit anti-clockwise. She looked forward to a long and mutually advantageous relationship.

I spent Wednesday wondering what explanation I could offer for my absence on Thursday before deciding in the end to offer none at all. I would simply leave the office shortly after lunch looking suitably purposeful, and return at five, after which I could easily make up the lost hours.

The truth was that my role – a senior economist with particular policy responsibility for both money laundering and European markets – would be demanding if I had not been doing it so long, and had not so effectively delegated most of the work to more junior employees. It is the dirty secret of management that, the more senior one becomes, the less work one actually does. The pressure on the Governor cannot be compared to that upon the graduate entrant in her second or third post.

In short, I would not be missed.

I walked anti-clockwise around the lake, I smoked, I returned to the office. At home I decided to phone for pizza – why not? By the time it was delivered another £100 had been transferred into my new account. I ate the pizza and the remaining cheesecake in celebration before wondering what, exactly, I was celebrating. Somebody once wrote that trying to die is not like trying to commit suicide, and might even be harder. Nonetheless, it must be done. I flushed this day my daily statin.

The following Tuesday – 10.00 a.m.: clockwise – would be a problem, however. It was the second Tuesday of the month, a fixed date in the Bank's calendar, the management board meeting. I could not simply walk out. I replied to Sarah, explaining that unfortunately the proposed time was not possible for me, and offering Monday or Wednesday mornings as alternatives. I would be as accommodating as I could, I wrote, but there were some commitments I simply could not avoid. There was no reply until, on Tuesday at 10.15 a.m., in the middle of the management meeting, I received a written disciplinary warning, including a statement of my misconduct that I was instructed to sign, scan and return.

Who did this woman think she was?

The Deputy Governor had spotted me scrolling through the screen of my smartphone. 'Anything important?'

It was not the sort of question that required an answer.

But, *honestly*, I thought. She's paid me £200. What was that? Less than I would earn by merely sitting through this interminable meeting, pretending to pay attention. It wasn't as if I needed the money – Sarah's or the Bank's, come to that. I had been here three decades, earning more than a man of moderate desires could possibly spend. I had no mortgage – the divorce settlement had paid for the flat – and our only child was already more grown up, and better paid, than I. Cigarettes and decent wine are expensive, but there's only so much one can consume alone. My pension would be more than enough to keep me in carcinogens until the day I died.

I was, in fact, already free.

That afternoon, I signed and returned the disciplinary statement.

Eventually, of course, my colleagues began to notice something was amiss. The Deputy Governor asked if everything was all right. I assured him that it was. A couple of weeks later, however, during which I had circumambulated the Serpentine a dozen times, I was summoned to meet the Director of Human Resources, a woman of about my own age who had only recently been recruited to the Bank. She had joined us, it was rumoured, from somewhere in the pharmaceutical industry.

'Denise Matthews,' she said, as if I might not know. 'Take a seat, Gordon. You don't mind if I call you Gordon?'

I did mind, but of course I did not say so.

'I won't beat about the bush,' she said, proceeding to do so. 'Your colleagues are worried about you, Gordon.'

'It's my wife,' I said, and saw her glance down quickly

at the folder on her desk. 'My ex-wife,' I corrected myself. 'Elaine.'

Ms Matthews waited. I waited, wondering what I might say next.

'She has cancer,' I said.

'I'm sorry to hear that, Gordon.'

'Of the oesophagus.'

Where had that come from? *Oesophagus* was a soft, plangent word I was sure I had not used since Mrs Catchpole's O-level Biology class, but which suited perfectly the mood I was trying to create. As a cancer, it was, moreover, both aggressive and relatively rare, reducing the chances of Denise Matthews having suffered the same condition, or knowing anybody else who had. I did not want to find myself comparing symptoms.

'I'm sorry,' she said again.

I was granted a month's leave of absence. After that, she said, we would review the situation.

'I'm sure a month will be more than enough,' I said mournfully.

It wasn't, though. Not only did Elaine remain stubbornly alive, but so – despite the significant increase in my intake of cigarettes and saturated fat – did I. Perhaps it was the exercise? Before long I was walking around the lake – and sometimes further afield: along the Mall, around Green Park and even, my own favourite, St James' Park – two or even three times every day. The money in my deposit account was mounting up – but to what end? And where was it coming from? My point about *Concrete* – my insight, I had termed it all those years ago – had been that Sarah Slother's mysterious inheritance would not be a disposable fortune, but a liability: that the crumbling pile would be the ruin of its new owner. I returned to the book – the house had been called Niederkreut, I found – and then to Google: Niederkreut did not exist. In the novel it was located a manageable walk from Rudolph's own house in the village of Peiskam, to which he had retreated from the overwhelming horrors of Vienna. Peiskam did not exist, either. But where, I wondered, had Thomas Bernhard himself lived? The answer was: Gmunden, a small town in Upper Austria, much frequented as a health and summer resort, where, after years of debilitating lung disease, he was finally assisted in his suicide at the age of fifty-eight: his home is now a considerable tourist attraction, featuring prominently on the website of the local tourist board, alongside a luxurious spa retreat set in the house and gardens of a sixteenth-century baronial hall. According to its own website, the spa specializes in helping visitors – the word patient is never used – to recover from addictions of many kinds. Abundant testimonials aver that confirmed smokers – those who, like me, have smoked forty cigarettes or more every day of their adult lives – leave the spa and never smoke again. Former opioid addicts remain drug-free. Even gamblers can lose the itch to stake all they have, and more. Far from a financial burden, the house that had once been Niederkreut is evidently now a veritable goldmine.

The following day – a heavy, humid afternoon towards the end of August – between the Round Pond and the Diana Memorial Playground, I spotted, some twenty yards ahead and walking slowly towards me, an elderly woman with a head of striking red hair. Halfway between us walked another, much younger, woman, attempting to light a cigarette. She stopped, cupping her hand around her lighter, although there was scarcely any breeze. The woman with the red hair stopped, too. I continued walking at my own steady pace. As I passed the younger woman, I caught her eye, and winked. I was not alone! For the rest of that hour, and during the two that followed, as the sky darkened, the air thickened and sweat began to gather uncomfortably in the creases of my clothes, I remained on the lookout for fellow strolling smokers. Sure enough, ten paces behind each one there strolled a woman, or a man, sometimes old, sometimes young, often neither. There we all were, parading in our silent pairs around the park, each dedicated smoker accompanied by his or her pale, passive-smoking shadow.

Towards the end of my third shift, there was a sudden clap of thunder and the tar-black skies finally opened. The hot rain felt like being pelted with soft, ripe fruit; we all, smokers and shadows alike, scurried for cover as best we could. I made it to the Sackler Gallery and took shelter under the extraordinary flopped-pancake roof. I looked around at my fellow refugees, one of whom was presumably my shadow. Was it the elderly gentleman with the linen suit and an elegant cane? Or the woman in a printed cotton dress and a soft leather jacket draped over her shoulders? She looked somehow familiar, and I realized that, far from being my shadow, she was the smoker I had seen struggling to light her cigarette. Should I speak to her? Before I could decide another thought struck me: if she were here, did that mean her shadow – the red-haired woman: *Sarah Slother* – was here, too? I glanced around again, trying not to attract too much attention, before realizing that the young woman would by now have changed shadows at least twice, as I had myself, since we'd first passed each other. There was no reason to suppose that Sarah Slother was there with us, outside the Sackler Gallery.

That weekend was the August Bank Holiday and, naturally, the weather remained unreliable. Elizabeth had emailed to say she would be in the country. She had reserved a table for the three of us for Sunday lunch, after which she would be able to stay with me until Monday evening. The three of us? She meant Elaine, to whose oesophageal cancer I realized, with a pang of guilt, I had given not a moment's thought. Would she be well enough? Could I face the prospect? The presence of illness, other than my own, always made me squeamish. Would I be available? I was on leave from the Bank, but had no idea whether, in my secondary employment as a smoker, I was entitled to statutory holidays. Consulting the contract I'd been sent, I found it silent on the subject. It was more than likely, I considered, when so many people had additional time on their hands, that demand for Sarah Slother's services would be particularly high. It appeared that hers was not a cottage industry, that out of the surprise bequest of Niederkreut she had built a substantial business, recruiting hundreds of active smokers to serve the needs of her health spa's addicted clients. But why London? She had clearly expanded into an international operation, but Bernhard was little known here, and much more highly regarded on the continent. Most likely, England was not the first, or even the second, but merely the latest invest- ment in a truly global venture. Other European capitals

– not to mention New York, of course, and Tokyo and Beijing – would likely boast their own networks of health spas and passive smoking services. The fellowship to which I now belonged was not limited to Hyde Park but spread its tendrils throughout the world. Behind every smoker was a shadow, paying handsomely for the nostalgic pleasure of second-hand smoke and making Sarah Slother, of 128 Knightsbridge, an address that did not exist, richer than the old cavalry officer could ever have dreamed.

I emailed Elizabeth to say that I might be called unexpectedly to work over the weekend. She might be better off remaining with her mother. She replied, telling me not to be ridiculous and not to be late for lunch.

In the event, I had no professional engagements on the Sunday and arrived at the restaurant ahead of time. Even after walking twice around the block, smoking a cigarette on my own time, as it were, I was still early. I went inside and explained that my daughter had made a reservation, for three. I asked for a quiet corner table, somewhere away from both the kitchens and the windows. This was going to be a difficult lunch. The maîtresse d' – a young woman half Elizabeth's age, let alone mine – explained that all guests ate at a communal table. It was Chef's mission, she said, to encourage conviviality, without which his food could not properly be appreciated. I ordered a large gin and tonic and was told that spirits were not served before the meal, as they distressed the taste buds. Determined not to lose this battle entirely, I ordered champagne.

'You do have wine, I take it?'

'Of course, sir.'

'Dom Perignon?'

'Unfortunately . . .'

Hah!

'Then bring me what you have,' I sighed, relieved.

The communal table was three-quarters full, and the champagne bottle half empty, by the time Elizabeth and her mother both arrived, jostling for precedence as they came through the restaurant door together. Elaine and I were divorced but not entirely separated. Elizabeth would not allow it, and it was mostly through Elizabeth that we communicated. We had spoken by telephone once or twice (about Elizabeth), but it had been three years – her father's funeral – since Elaine and I had actually met. I had always admired her father and saw in our divorce no reason to deprive myself of the pleasure of seeing him interred. Elaine was magnificent that day, greeting me – and even kissing the air beside my cheek – as if I were some colleague of her father's who had occasionally visited to play bezique when she was growing up, and whose name she could not quite remember. I had never loved her more. Now, as she handed her light coat to the maîtresse d', I saw that she had lost none of her imperious charm. The old scar where her temple had collided with the broken glass was invisible beneath her fringe. She looked remarkably good, I thought, for a woman undergoing chemotherapy.

'My God, Gordon,' she said. 'You look grey.'

I ran my hand through my hair, which I could not deny had been getting thinner of late. 'It happens,' I said. 'My father was as white as a polar bear at my age.'

Elizabeth said, 'Not your hair, Dad. Your face.'

I rubbed my cheek, as if some of the offending pigment might come off on my fingers.

'I'm fine,' I said. 'Would you like champagne?'

Having arrived early, I had been able to stake a claim to one corner of the only table, reducing the risk of interaction with our fellow diners. However, the consequence, I now realized, was that while we did not have to sit in a row like three wise monkeys, or shout to each other across the broad, bare planks of faux-rustic oak, Elaine and Elizabeth would naturally sit one on either side, with me the centre of attention. This was not how I had envisaged lunch.

'Who are you seeing?' Elaine asked, which I had also not anticipated.

'No one,' I said. 'You know . . . Not since.' Since her. Since the divorce. 'How about you?'

'I meant a doctor, Gordon. Are you still with What's-his-name?'

Dr Wistermane was the consultant cardiologist I'd been referred to when the blood drained from our GP's face at the sight of my cholesterol results.

'Off and on,' I said. 'Shall we order?'

'You don't order here, Dad.'

'We don't?'

'We eat whatever Chef prepares. Don't worry, you'll love it.'

I thought I would hate it. Not the food, about which I was prepared to keep an open mind, but the loss of control. Placing myself in the hands of an autocratic stranger. A month before, I would have hated it. But now I found there was a certain pleasure in relinquishing responsibility. Was this what finally dying would be like, I wondered? I had been trying for so long. In the event, the food proved exceptionally good, and the wine was at least adequate to the occasion. When I had drunk enough to summon up the courage, I asked: 'Why are we here?' Sat in the middle, I saw a look of urgent complicity pass between mother and daughter, a brief nod. A decision had been reached.

From my left, Elaine said, 'Elizabeth was worried about you.'

'Isn't it our job to worry about Elizabeth?'

Not that we ever had, or needed to.

From my right: 'You're not well, Dad.'

'I'm fine.'

I was not fine. I'd lost my wife. I'd lost Elaine. And yet Elaine was here. I turned to her. 'It's you,' I said.

I saw her eyes flick away, towards the maîtresse d'. 'What's me, Gordon?'

'It's you who has *cancer.*'

My stage whisper was loud enough for the silence that followed to spread around the long, shared table.

'Not me,' I added.

Elaine spoke quietly, the way she used to when she was disappointed in me. 'I don't have cancer, Gordon.'

Of course she didn't.

I laughed. 'Of course you don't,' I said. 'I just forgot, for a moment . . .'

'Forgot?'

The Bank, the HR Director. Elaine was sitting next to me, finishing her dessert. I'd forgotten I'd invented her cancer to excuse my absences from work. I couldn't explain that, not to Elaine.

'I've decided to stop work,' I said. 'To leave the Bank.'

Another glance passed across the corner of the table.

'That might be for the best.'

Elizabeth seemed more concerned. 'When did you decide this, Dad?'

In truth, when I'd opened my mouth.

'About a month ago,' I said.

'Well, good for you,' Elaine said. 'I'm sure you can afford it.'

And there it was, I swear: the bitter taint in her voice. Honestly. It wasn't as if I'd made off with all the money. Or even half the money. I had what I needed: a flat, that was all. The prospect of a pension. A broken table. She had the rest. It wasn't as if I'd run off with, with, with – what was the word she'd used? – with a fucking *ceramicist*.

'What's the matter?' I said. 'Pots not selling?'

'Gordon . . .'

'I'm sorry. I'm sorry, I'm sorry. I'm so sorry.'

She hadn't run off. I hadn't run off. Nobody had run off. With anything, with anybody. That wasn't how it happened. She hadn't. I—

'I'd better leave.'

'Dad?'

I left.

Outside, I lit a cigarette. Where was I?

Clerkenwell.

What on earth was I doing in Clerkenwell? I would walk towards the City. This new development required thought. If I were going to leave the Bank, I'd need to consider my other source of income. I needed to take my new career more seriously. I couldn't be here, wherever I was now, wasting time. I should be in Hyde Park, smoking. But was it just Hyde Park? Were all Sarah Slother's London clients based in – or at least summoned to – the

West End? Passing Bart's Hospital I spotted a man lighting a cigarette without breaking his slow but steady stride.
Sure enough, ten paces behind him, a woman pushing an
expensive baby stroller sniffed the air. We were everywhere.
We were pictures in the smokers' attics. We had no need
to be afraid.

I was not afraid.

I have always found the City particularly restorative
at weekends. It is not simply that there are so few people,
or that the majority of shops and even the pubs and cafés
still close for the Sabbath, but that the air itself is somehow
stilled, silenced.

What happened was that I'd hit her. My wife. Elaine.
I hit my wife. And she had fallen into the broken glass.

In the stillness, the mediaeval bones of the city's tiny,
knotted alleyways poked through the steel and tinted glass,
while its breath – a blend of wood smoke, river mud and
horse dung – exhaled from the ancient lungs of Poultry,
Cheapside, Garlick Hill and Pudding Lane.

Once. It would never happen again, I said; she must
know that. Yes, she said, she knew, but still she had to leave.
And she was right. Once . . . The table was shattered. One
cannot live with a man who has done that.

There *was* a ceramicist, but that had never been the
point. He was never more than retaliation, I know that.

Tourists thronged Paternoster Row as thickly as ever,
photographing themselves against a cathedral background.

She'd brought home one of his *pieces*. It was curved,
with a deep glaze, blue, shading into a fathomless black;
it caught the light and didn't let go. I asked what it was
supposed to *be*. She laughed and called me a philistine.

What do you think it is, she asked. Neither use nor ornament, I replied, as she placed it carefully on the Japanese glass-topped coffee table we'd bought at Harrods to mark our twentieth anniversary.

By the time I returned home, there was a message from Elizabeth complaining that I never answered my mobile, and an email from Sarah Slother booking me for two slots the following morning, three more in the afternoon. Smokers' shadows clearly had no respect for statutory holidays after all. When Elizabeth arrived, later that evening, I told her I was on my way to bed: I had to be up early in the morning and she would have to fend for herself. I had warned her, I said.

It was a relief to be working again.

On Tuesday I carried Elizabeth's diminutive suitcase to the taxi and waved her off. I'd be all right, I assured her. I was fine.

My leave of absence from the Bank came to an end, but I did not return. Just after nine one morning, there was a knock at the door. I pulled my dressing gown around me – I had no engagements until after lunch – padded in my slippers down the stairs and opened the door to find Denise Matthews holding a briefcase.

'You're on my way to work,' she said – which I doubted but saw no advantage in disputing. 'Can I come in?'

What possible reason could I give for refusing? I made my way back up the stairs, allowing her to follow me. I directed her towards the living room and offered coffee. I hoped she would stay put, allowing me an opportunity to gather my thoughts while the kettle boiled, but she followed me into the kitchen, talking brightly about the state of my flat, about Elaine, about the Bank. She used the words *duty of care*. Back in the living room I warned her to watch out for the coffee table, the sprawling ebony supports of which reached up, like the exposed ribs of an abandoned boat left rotting on the beach, towards empty air. She would not have been the first to miss the absence of the shattered glass.

'What happened?'

I didn't answer. One cannot live with a man who has done that.

Denise sat down still holding her mug, then placed it carefully on the floor beside her chair. She opened her briefcase and took out a sheaf of papers. She hoped I would agree, she said. It was for the best, all round.

I signed where she indicated I should sign.

'I have cancer,' I said, 'of the oesophagus. It's for the best.'

Today is my fifty-eighth birthday. Fifty-eight was enough for Bernhard. I have spent the morning strolling around the Serpentine, treating my shadows to some particularly fine Virginia tobacco that I'd found online, confident that they would appreciate the gesture. I returned home to find an email from Elizabeth and a birthday card from Elaine – the first for several years – in which she has written that she hopes I will look after myself.

It is harder, but it must be done.

She hopes I might find a way of living that is not just kinder to others, but to myself. It is important, she writes, for me to try.

◊

The final passage of the story – if that is what it is – is dated October, 2019. Six months later, already hospitalized, my father contracted COVID-19, and died. Whether it was the virus that killed him remains an open question.

Elizabeth Hanbury
April, 2026

A Day Like Any Other

Tuesday, 11.30 a.m.

KEVIN LET HIMSELF in this morning, just as I closed the bedroom door. I wish he wouldn't. I've told him often enough – told him not to come at all, in fact – but you would insist on giving him a key. In case you weren't around, you said. In which case I could let him in myself, I said, although I honestly can't see why I should. You said he's my oldest friend. That doesn't mean I want him fossicking around me like a squirrel hoarding nuts.

He asks about the scratches on my face, and I tell him I've been clumsy shaving. I tell him he's just missed you, which is true enough, and that you'd gone to yoga.

'Isn't she marvellous?'

I don't answer.

'Eighty, and still yoga-ing.'

'We're eighty, Kevin. Not Ellen.'

'Well, near as makes no difference.'

It makes no difference now.

He's come bearing biscuits: stem ginger, coated in dark

chocolate. Very moreish, I say. He says I shouldn't eat them all at once.

'That's not what's going to kill me.'

He gets that look he gets, and says: 'I suppose.'

I'm just waiting for him to go, so I can tidy up here. I eat one with the coffee that I let him bring up to me, just to be polite.

I have stockpiled and kept my powders dry, ready, against the day.

One day.

Not *one day*. Today.

He says, 'We should leave some for Ellen.'

There is a fly crawling around the window above the desk – on the outside, I mean. It is January and the fly has no right being there. Or anywhere, really. A winter sun is shining, however, and the fly warms itself on the white stucco windowsill, rubbing its legs as if to restore its circulation. (Does a fly's blood circulate? I suppose it must.) When it walks across the glass, its belly lights up orange and translucent in the sunshine. It too will be dead by teatime.

For years I have teetered on the precipice of type-2 diabetes, never quite toppling over, but edging close enough for a succession of doctors and allied health professionals to warn me dourly to avoid sugar, cut down on carbs and definitely, definitely not to exceed fourteen units of alcohol a week. I nod sagely, acknowledging the wisdom of their words, but keep my own counsel.

I eat the biscuits Kevin has left behind, sweep the crumbs into the wastepaper bin.

Is Kevin my oldest friend? Aside from my sister Jean, he is certainly the person I've known longest on this planet. We were at primary school together. He wasn't there to begin with, then he was. His parents must have moved house, or he'd been expelled from somewhere else. He was annoying enough. He turned up just before the eleven plus. But then he followed me to grammar school and never left.

I don't know why. He says he doesn't, either. I told him to go away many times, to fuck off and not come back, but somehow he always did, even when I backed up my words with fists and kicks. He was bigger than me. Still is, of course. But big is relative. A big dog isn't necessarily bigger than a person, it just has a look in its eye that says it could clamp its teeth into your throat, then yank and shake until, finally, you stop twitching. Kevin, on the other hand, is big the way a cow is big. Or a manatee. Large and placid. When I punched him, my knuckles sank into pale flesh like uncooked pastry. I never got the sense that he felt any pain. He certainly never punched me back.

You liked him. I tried to keep the two of you apart, but with Kevin that just wasn't possible. He was my best man, when we finally got married.

What a day that was!

When Maddy died a couple of years ago, after fifty years of being Kevin's wife – more than enough for anyone, I'd have thought – he acted the inconsolable widower for a while: *It should have been me!* Boo-hoo. Then he met a man in a pub who really turned him around, he said. Well, maybe. Or perhaps he read it in a magazine somewhere, or on the internet: with Kevin it is never wise to put much faith in anything he says. He lies about the strangest things, and his stories tend to fall apart completely in the lightest breeze. He must have got the idea somewhere, though, he wouldn't have come up with it himself. So okay, then, let's say: from a man he met in a pub who had read it in a book or magazine or on a website, maybe, or had heard it himself from a second man in another pub, and, in any case, passed it on to Kevin, who passed it on to me, like a virus.

– *Do you feel bad, Kevin?* the man had asked.

– *Of course,* said Kevin.

– *Would you want Maddy to suffer the way you're suffering now?*

And naturally Kevin would have said, or thought he'd say:

– *No, no! I'd give my life to spare her that!*

– *But don't you see,* the man, or magazine, continued, complacently, *that's just what you* are *doing! Living on after Maddy is the greatest gift you could ever offer. The only way to spare her the grief of bereavement.*

– *That's true,* said Kevin, greatly consoled, until he told me about it later, and I said: 'Unless you'd died together.'

'How do you mean?'

'Like a plane crash,' I said. 'Or a fire.'

'True,' Kevin said, 'but what are the odds of that?'

'Or a suicide pact.'

'Oh, now. No, no. Maddy would never have agreed to that.'

'I suppose not.'

'You suppose not. Would Ellen?'

He spoke angrily, self-righteously. What could I say? I said, 'No, no. Not Ellen.'

What kind of fly has a translucent belly? It looked normal from above. A housefly. I could look it up, I suppose, but I honestly don't care enough. If it is a housefly, it has nonetheless got outside the house somehow. Where has it been all winter?

Now Davie has come. Will there be no end to it?

I can hear him at the door, calling through the letterbox. Davie does not have his own key, despite being my son; he comes far less often than Kevin, even now. I have not been downstairs in months. I will have to use the stairlift.

Davie knows that I am dying, he just does not understand when. He is too young to understand the difference between *one* day and *a* day, like any other, like today. When the doctors say we cannot know with any certainty, he believes them.

2.00 p.m.

Back upstairs. The lift is manageable, with wheelchairs located top and bottom.

I thought he'd never leave. I told him you must have gone shopping, after your yoga.

He said you needn't have bothered. He could have done the shopping for you, if we'd only let him know. As it was, he had brought only cake, and brandy.

I told him you'd probably have lunch in town: he shouldn't wait.

Davie is not young. He had a fiftieth birthday party once. You said it didn't seem possible. I said that's just what happens when you hang around long enough. It happened to us, after all. You said you couldn't believe we had a child who was fifty, and when you put it like that, it does seem odd. Like those mediaeval paintings where the Holy Infant appears to be an irritable middle-manager, only small.

It wasn't much of a party. There were six of us, in a park, because those were the rules at the time. Davie's always been one for rules. His teacher said he'd put his hand up to speak in class, and could we ask him not to, please? I asked why she couldn't tell him this herself and she said they were keen to nurture an informal vibe where children felt comfortable exploring who they were. It would have been the seventies, of course. You thought Davie was just being polite. I said he was seven and could do without exploring who he was for a few years yet – or forever, with a bit of luck. He has not been lucky, as it turns out, even though we moved him out of that school and, later, sent him miles away, where there were still grammar schools like the one I went to, where teachers ignored their pupils, and beat them with canes if they spoke up in class. They never caned Davie, as far as I know.

We met up on Jesus Green, for the party. It's not quite local for any of us, so technically, not actually within the rules in any case. I didn't mention this to Davie. It would only have worried him and he might have called the whole thing off. He shouldn't be alone, you said, not on his fiftieth. When I let it slip out, though, after something Kevin said, Davie started looking round for cops, as if they might be hiding in the bushes. He'd seen videos on Facebook where the police filmed people walking in the countryside and later fined them.

'Dad,' said Rachel, Davie's daughter, 'I know it's hard these days, but maybe you should get out more?'

The six of us were you and me; Davie, of course, and Davie's children, Rachel and Jake, who are grown up now, with degrees and jobs and flats and flatmates they say they hate; and Kevin.

Who invites his godfather to a fiftieth birthday party? A man whose wife has recently left him, that's who. Because if she hadn't, we'd have been six without Kevin, and he couldn't have come anyway.

Maddy wasn't at the party, on account of there being six of us, and, well, said Davie, rules were rules. When it came time to leave, though, it turned out she'd been there all along, parked up across the river, powering through sudokus and listening to Radio 3. She'd been fine, she said. It had been nice to get a couple of hours to herself. It must have been just after that she found the lump. By the time she died, I think we were allowed thirty people at a funeral, but I'm not sure. There weren't thirty of us, anyway; sitting two metres apart was not a problem.

When did you and I first meet? I know it was an afternoon, about teatime, in the summer of 1962. It was probably July, towards the end of the month. But I couldn't say what day. A day in most respects no different from the one before, or the one after. The sun was definitely shining, like today, but much more brightly. This is not just nostalgia: the sun shone a great deal that summer. I had recently finished university: Chemistry, at Nottingham, not out of any real desire to be a chemist, but in the hope of deferring National Service. There was talk in the air that it might be abolished.

(It was.)

The winter after that glorious summer would be the coldest since the one in 1947 that Dad always banged on about. He said we didn't know we were born, Jean and me, even though I'd have been six and can clearly remember icicles the size of hockey sticks and people skating on the frozen fields. He said my Aunt Dot – whose actual name was Frances, but who was about two-foot-six, he always said, both wide and high, and who lived with us and looked after me and Jean when our mother died, killed by a V2 while he fought his way through the Ardennes, he said – Aunty Dot slipped and fell through the ice in the Forty Foot drain one night on her way back from cleaning the church my father never attended. She couldn't get out – her arms were too short, you see, Dad said, tucking his elbows in and flapping his palms like a Tyrannosaurus Rex – and as the night wore on the ice re-froze around her neck. It was a wonder she survived, he said. A miracle, Dot always said, with a wink. My father snorted. He wouldn't call a drunken verger falling in on top of her a miracle.

Jean never believed a word of it, but she'd have been about two at the time, so what did she know? Aunt Dot had something wrong with her kidneys and died at the end of my first year at Nottingham. I had exams and had to miss the funeral. She told me once the reason the Doodlebug killed our mother and not us was that she'd been in another man's flat at the time.

I said technically it wasn't a Doodlebug, which was the V1. It was a V2 that killed Mum. Didn't she know anything?

Perhaps a little of that cake Davie brought? Can't hurt.

4.30 p.m.

The day is slipping away. If I'm not careful it will be gone, like all the others.

I didn't mean to write about my mother, or Aunt Dot, or the war, but about when I met you. It seems appropriate, today. The most important day of my life, and I couldn't tell you when it was, exactly, which is my point. One day, a day – a summer's day, sixty years ago. I can see you clearly, though, in a patterned cotton dress and a delicate cardigan that matched your eyes, climbing the stile and walking towards my tree, that wasn't my tree at all. It was an old oak on what passed for high ground in those parts – a gently sloping mound just outside the village with a drop of maybe six feet to the north. I used to sit under its branches and read poetry when I was feeling soulful. I'd smoked my first cigarette there, drunk my first bottle of Bass. Your hair was dark, curls cut short still sprang unruly round your face. I said hello. You sat beside me and said this was your tree, too. I said I hadn't seen you before. Which, if you'd grown up in a village in the Fens, you'd have known wasn't just a chat-up line. There was no one you didn't recognize.

Your eyes were – are – the deepest blue imaginable, like a stained-glass sky, or the Madonna's robe. Your shoes were brown and sturdy, with thick heels and heavy laces, practical for walking in the fields.

You hadn't grown up here, you said. Your family moved south two years ago. Your father worked for the Drainage Board.

I'd been away, I said, at university. I lingered on the word. I had little idea what to do with my degree; but impressing a beautiful girl might just be one thing it was good for.

You said you'd finished school a week ago. You were going to college, too, in the autumn. You would be eighteen then.

'Secretarial?'

You smiled indulgently. 'Classics. At Girton.'

I hadn't applied to Cambridge. Because I wanted to get away from home, not potter into the city on the same bus I'd taken to school for seven years. But I hadn't applied to Oxford, either. *Things are changing in this country, boys,* my teachers said, managing our expectations. *The red bricks are where the real science is being done.*

I said, 'Then you'll be living at home?'

'I will not.'

Later that evening, when I asked about new faces in the village, my father didn't have a clue, but Jean did. She said everybody did: Head Girl, first violin in the school orchestra, Clytemnestra in the Sixth Form end-of-year production. There was no getting away from Ellen Underhill.

'Who's Clytemnestra?'

'You don't want to know.'

And yes, her father worked for the Drainage Board, but he was their Chief Engineer or something, he wasn't digging ditches.

'Out of your league,' Jean said, summing up.

'Then how come I'm taking her to the pictures at the weekend?'

'I don't know. Did you drug her?'

'That's enough,' Dad said. 'Haven't you got homework?'

Jean rolled her eyes and said it was the summer holidays. Dad gave up on her and asked me what I was doing to find a job.

'Applying to the Drainage Board,' Jean said. 'So he can marry the boss's daughter.'

She went up to her room before Dad could tell her to, and I said I thought I was due a bit of a break after three years at university. There'd be time enough to sort out the rest of my life.

From where I'm sitting, in the quiet room we call the study – not that I ever studied here – I can see not only dying flies but back gardens full of long-dead wet grey leaves, dropped months ago by sycamore trees with ivy-throttled trunks; I see pocket lawns and muddy, colourless borders, separated by more or less decrepit fences. Next door have had the builders in since before the pandemic started; they could have built a whole new house in less time than they've spent knocking theirs about. Right now, there's a man with a shovel standing in their garden, up to his armpits in a hole big enough to bury two people side-by-side. It occurs to me I haven't seen the neighbours for a while. I don't really imagine they're going to wind up under the new patio, but it would make a delicious end to a lockdown story.

You would have laughed.

It's good that Davie's kids still keep in touch with their father. There was a time, after he lost his job and said he couldn't pay the maintenance, when his ex-wife said in that case, he couldn't see them. I'm pretty sure it was that way round, although I also remember him losing a job when he got involved in some sort of dispossessed dads' demonstration and chained himself to the scaffolding around the clock tower on the town hall. Which was a total aberration, for Davie, who follows the rules and doesn't usually do things like that. Or like anything, really, except come around, like Kevin, but less often.

I need a pee. These days, it's quite a performance.

For years, there was a knack to flushing the downstairs toilet properly in this house, or the cistern would just keep pouring water into the bowl forever. I'd have to lift the lid and fiddle around with the ballcock. You said we should get it fixed; I said it was just a knack. If people would only flush it the way I did – the way I'd *told* them to – there wouldn't be a problem. Then one day I came home, and you had fixed it.

I said it wouldn't last.

'I called a plumber.'

'Who needs a plumber? It's just a knack.'

Maybe my train had been delayed that day by some inconsiderate bastard on the tracks. I usually knew better.

You said, 'It's done.'

'It'll be a waste of money and won't make any difference.'

'I mean, it's *done*. There was a plumber working two doors down who popped in this afternoon. It's fixed.'

I didn't believe you of course. It wouldn't last. But I had to break the fucking thing myself to make the point.

There's a knack to it, I said, after that, when I'd calmed down.

6.00 p.m.

It was your study, really. You often worked at home. Even when you retired, you never really stopped. Why should you? You could still read and write, you said. What else would you do?

Your translation of *Elektra* caught a wave of media interest in women classicists. I don't pretend to understand why, but I was happy for you.

When I retired, I retired.

Kevin always told the most ridiculous lies. Lies so palpably false they weren't really lies at all, but some other art form altogether. If challenged, he'd back down, step by step, never acknowledging any contradiction. I remember one about the time he and his dad went shark fishing in Mexico, when I knew for a fact he'd never in his life been anywhere there wasn't a Lyons Corner House. He said the boat had one of those big rotating chairs, like at the barber's, all padded leather arms, with a hole for a cold drink you could sip while hauling on the rod that slotted into a socket between your feet: his dad had borrowed it, the boat, from a friend Kevin wasn't supposed to know smuggled dope into the Florida Keys. I nodded along, enjoying the ride. But a day or two later, back at school, I picked away at the loose ends, watching the story unravel. The sport-fishing boat became a dinghy with an outboard the size of a wardrobe, then a rowing boat; the Great White devolved into a basking shark, then a baby basking shark washed up dead on a beach in Dorset, not Mexico. All harmless enough, like most of

Kevin's fabrications, I suppose, and just as flimsy. But I felt obliged, for his own good, to bring him down a little closer to earth.

Davie cannot recognize what he's looking at. I am his future, but he isn't old enough to see it. Of course he knows, the way everybody knows, that he'll die one day. Which is to say, by not knowing it at all. *One day* is not a real day. It's a hypothetical day, a long way off. A day that exists only in a parallel universe in which he can be not alive. A thought experiment he can afford to play around with. It is not, as it is for me, and for you, Ellen, a day like any other.

Like today.

When the doctors said there was no hope – when had there ever been? I said, trying to lighten the mood – you said you wouldn't do it.

'Do what?'

'You don't remember?'

Of course I did. I knew perfectly well I'd told you, more than once, that if I ever got a terminal diagnosis, or just became too much to live with, you were to put a pillow over my face and sit on it until I soiled the sheets and my pallid corpse stopped twitching. But that had been before Maddy, before Kevin's magazine or book or man in a bar. It wasn't the mercy killing I could not now ask of you. It was the grief of living afterwards. Without me.

You didn't promise anything at the time. You didn't say you wouldn't, either. But only because you didn't think I meant it.

'It's always all or nothing with you, isn't it?'

That's what you said instead.

'Life isn't like that,' you said. 'In this world, everything's a mess. This and that, all muddled up. Not one thing then another. We have to pick our way through.'

Those would be your last words on the subject, you said, then.

But years later, when I wasn't even asking, you came right out and said you wouldn't do it. It was the very first thing you said when the doctor left the room and before the nurses came to get me ready to go home.

You cried, though. When you got your voice back under control, you said that you'd cried the first time, too, even though you didn't really think I'd meant it. You had cried because I'd said it anyway.

How could I ever leave a woman like you all alone?

11.00 p.m.

Some people think you shouldn't say 'I love you' all the time. That it cheapens real emotion, like a pop song. I've never gone along with that.

One probably shouldn't say it too soon, though. The first time I ever did, the girl replied, 'I'm sorry.' Which I dare say she was, but that's not what anybody wants to hear. She hugged me, or allowed me to hug her. I can't remember which. We didn't kiss. I cycled home singing a sad song aloud but to myself.

It was different with you, though.

Sometimes one knows. You knew, I'm sure, although you were determined to complete your degree and start a career.

When Davie came along it wouldn't – couldn't – ever be the same, but mostly it was better. I can honestly say that. When he grew up and left home, that was better, too, in a different way.

Just you and me. And Kevin, I suppose. Like in the beginning.

I have nothing against Kevin, not really. Or Davie either, come to that. It's just, their coming here, today, made me pretend it wasn't happening. Which only reminds me that it has.

I had to do it while I still retained the strength. While I could get out of the bedroom, close the door and wheel myself to the bathroom, alone, unhindered by your hand on my arm, clutching at my face, tearing the brittle skin for the first time in decades.

Kevin never punched me back; you never had cause. Not really.

You twitched, until you didn't.

The doctors don't bother warning me off alcohol and sugar anymore. One nurse even says at this stage a little of what I fancy can't do me any harm. As if she were my mother, or at least Aunt Dot.

Davie doesn't quite say that. He doesn't have to: he brought cake and brandy.

But I no longer want them. Not all of Kevin's lies were harmless, I see now. Now that it's too late, I find I want – I need – to keep myself healthy, or at least alive, for as long as my mis-firing genes allow. Not as a service, not as a gift, as Kevin's book or magazine or drunken interlocutor would have it, but because it is the least that I deserve, after all I've done.

I'll flush my hoarded powder down the toilet I broke and you had fixed, again.

Keep going.

It's the least that I deserve.

The Tardigrade

I T'S BEEN A while, love. What can I tell you?

They moved me here a year ago. As you can see, my office has two windows, neither of which provides any natural light. The one immediately behind overlooks me from the Hub; the other, directly opposite and in my line of sight whenever I gaze up from my computer screen, looks out onto the Hangar. There is a face pressed against this second window. It is always possible there might be a face at the window behind me, too, but I can never know for sure because both windows are in fact one-way mirrors. I can no more see into the Hub than Hickox – whose lips and nose it is that work their way across my window like a sucker fish in an aquarium – can see into my office from the Hangar. Yet he knows I'm here and knows that I can see him. Knows, too, that I could dock his wages for this incivility – a week's worth, if I had the mind. Knows also that I won't. The bureaucratic repercussions are just not worth the minimal satisfaction it might offer.

When I say Hickox knows I'm here, you shouldn't take that literally. He knows that there is *someone* here. He may even know my name, if he has the wit to connect the position of the window overlooking his sector with the daily memoranda he receives concerning performance targets, health and safety infringements and team building events. He might even be able to put a face to that name, if he has ever bothered with the Comms team news page. (And if he believes the photographs displayed there correspond to the managers named. Which, by and large, they do.) He does not, however, know *me*. There is some comfort in that at least.

By the same token, of course, I do not know Jennifer Radley, who may or may not at this moment be observing me through the window immediately behind my desk. I tend to assume, however, that she has more valuable things to do with her time. Otherwise, I might go mad.

It is afternoon. I have eaten lunch – the price of a salad is charged to my account whether I take it or not – and drunk my afternoon cup of tea, but, still, it's much too early to go home. Now that you're no longer there, what remains? Our daughter, whom you named Ruth and who, indeed, pities me. Your father, both the cause and scourge of my timidity, as you once put it. When you died, he said he knew exactly how I felt. Which was not unreasonable; he too is a widower, after all. But he told me to get back out there. Time of my life, he said, and actually winked. While the cat's away, he said. I told him you were dead, not at a sales conference in Wrexham. Exactly, he said. As if that made any sense.

What else? A dog. Not Alfie, who, as you know, died shortly before your own diagnosis, but, still, I walk your father's dog most days, when he's not feeling up to it. It's a terrier of some sort, but I dare say you know that, too.

I think Jennifer Radley must observe me, sometimes. Now, for instance, with Hickox still slobbering on my window, a message pops up on my screen. A picture of a tardigrade. I reply with a cry-laugh emoji, despite the fact that I am neither laughing nor crying. Does Jennifer Radley know that tardigrades are virtually indestructible? That, when threatened by their environment, they enter a death-like state – it's called cryptobiosis – which involves expelling all the water from their bodies and curling up into a tiny, desiccated pellet? Does she believe Hickox is indestructible? Or that I am?

Of course not. She simply thinks that tardigrades look funny, and that Hickox – who, you will have noticed, is decidedly obese, with short arms and disproportionately tiny facial features set in a flat, round face – looks uncannily *like* a tardigrade, especially when he presses that ill-favoured face up against the snot-smeared glass of the window opposite the window behind my desk from which Jennifer Radley was – and may now *be* – observing us both.

I worry about the cry-laugh emoji, and follow it with a separate message to which I attach last week's media monitoring stats. There has been a modest uptick in page views/click-throughs, bucking seasonal expectations, and I have been saving this news against the day. Given the uncertainty regarding Jennifer Radley's intentions in sending me a picture of a tardigrade while a member of my team, who undoubtedly resembles a tardigrade, licks my office window, right now seems an auspicious moment to deploy such positive evidence of our progress.

No, love. Jennifer Radley has not replied. It is possible that she is no longer there. Or that she is there but has refocussed her attention on more important and/or urgent issues, such as a message from a VP, perhaps, or even from the CEO himself. Or that she is there, and has read my message, but does not feel it requires a response, despite the good news it contains. She may feel that withholding the anticipated response will unsettle me, thus motivating me to motivate the team, of which Hickox is the longest-standing member, to ever greater efforts. If this, rather than simple prior-itization, is indeed her reason for not responding to my second message, then she is right, insofar as the effect *is* to unsettle me. But as to the supposed motivational effects of such anxiety, I have to say she has another think coming. I'm surprised that somebody like Jennifer Radley could make such a simple, schoolboy error, until you point out that I have no evidence she has done so, other than my own supposition. Who's the schoolboy now? you ask.

I look at the small digital clock in the bottom right-hand corner of my screen. At least another hour and twenty minutes must pass before I can even begin to consider clos-ing my computer down and going home to Ruth and your father, and your father's dog.

Perhaps I should reprimand Hickox after all?

What do you think, love?

It would be something to do.

Crossing the Rubicon

December 28th, 11 p.m.

ONE DOWN, EIGHTY-NINE to go. It was all a bit of a rush, in the event. The call-up letter only came with the last-minute Christmas cards and the annual round-up from Gerald's sister in the USA. I'd have expected a bit more notice, although I can't say I was altogether sorry to leave the festivities unfinished. As usual, there were only the three of us, but Gerald insists on turkey and ham, and roast beef on Boxing Day. None of which Clare eats.

The accommodation here is comfortable enough, in a John Lewis kind of way, although I dare say the lack of natural light will become a problem when the days outside get longer. The SAD-lamps on the desk and by the sofa hardly make up for losing sight of the sky, but I suppose it could be worse. I could be in one of those nuclear submarines, whose commanders I wrote to today.

This is the one decision all Prime Ministers still know in advance they'll have to take, so I had a bit of time to think about it. Everyone says it's also the most consequential, but I soon realized it isn't, that it really doesn't matter. Unless a world war breaks out in the next three months, no one will ever know. All the same, I'm not allowed to reveal what I wrote, not even here, though no one will read this, either, for years after I'm no longer PM – after I'm dead, in all likelihood – and my instructions have been superseded many times. Margot was very clear on this point, during my induction.

I could have written: *Just toss a coin, boys!*

(Heads: obliterate St Petersburg. Tails: head south and hope a nuclear winter isn't as bad as it's cracked up to be.)

I'm not saying that I did. Just that I *could have*. No one would know.

December 29th – 8.30 a.m.

Slept like a log last night, which I have to say I wasn't expecting. Uneasy rests the head, and all that. But the mattress is the right sort of firm, and the duvet/pillow/linen set just lovely. Goose down, if I'm not mistaken; Egyptian cotton.

Also, I haven't really started yet. In most jobs, the first few days are exhausting. Even if you're not doing anything, you're somewhere new, meeting hordes of people, apologizing in advance for not remembering their names. Here, there's the flat, of course, but that didn't take long, and I only met one person all day: Margot.

I think I'm going to like Margot – which is just as well! She reminds me a little of Gerald, the way he was when we first started going out: one of those fearsomely clever but self-deprecating types the Civil Service used to pride itself on back when it still believed it was the best in the world.

Less so of Clare, although they must be about the same age.

6.30 p.m.

Well, I am blooded, so to speak. I have taken my first real decision.

It wasn't all that hard.

After breakfast, with something of a fanfare, Margot presented me with a battered red attaché case. Inside, a single sheet of paper, mostly blank: a one-sentence statement of the issue; a question; tick-boxes labelled Yes and No; a space for my signature. Margot explained all future decision requests would take this form. I should not ask for further information; she would offer no clarification, comment or opinion. She would return in an hour for my decision; if I needed longer, it would usually be possible. On this occasion, however, there was a deadline: the deportation flight was scheduled for ten-thirty.

Gerald used to shout at the radio when anyone put the case for Political Purity. He said it was childish and insulting to suggest that professional civil servants would manipulate inexperienced civilian Prime Ministers. The "Deep State" was nothing but a conspiracy theory; the "Establishment" just another word for people who knew what they were talking about. Every decision has a context, he said. You have to understand the nuances, balance the consequences, accept the lesser evil. For that you need more to go on than your gut: you need proper advice. What's more, he said, you have to listen to it. That's why he'd actually supported the change to Sortition in the first place. Because, he said, the old system gave politicians an incentive *not* to listen. To pretend that there were simple answers to difficult questions. But then, naturally, they had to go and muck it up.

The trouble with simple Yes/No questions, he said, is you get stupid answers.

Clare said the Sortition Referendum was a Yes/No question, wasn't it?

And she was right of course, for once.

Clare voted No.

When Margot left, I re-read the paper for form's sake, ticked "Yes", and signed my name. It did not take an hour; it hadn't taken a minute.

Like I say, it wasn't hard.

January 4th

There's a lot of down time in this job.

There is a television in the sitting room with a small collection of DVDs; I am not allowed broadcast TV, for fear that the news or documentaries or discussion of current affairs might affect the purity of my judgment. All the films are at least fifty years old, which seems to me naïve: as if what's right and wrong might change in fifty years!

I'd seen most of them before I met Gerald.

This afternoon I re-watched an absurdly youthful Dustin Hoffman reject an older married woman in favour of her daughter. Anne Bancroft was thirty-five when she played Mrs Robinson; at thirty-five, I was pregnant with Clare. Gerald was fifty. The film has not aged well.

I can have more DVDs, Margot says: anything I like, provided they're at least half a century old and not overtly political.

There is also a shelf of books: the Bible, the Quran, a Collected Shakespeare – as if I were on a desert island, I say, and Margot smiles – plus assorted paperbacks, all from comfortably before the invention of sexual intercourse.

I shall try a few pages of Hardy before I go to sleep; I haven't read *The Mayor of Casterbridge* since my time at university.

January 11th

Today: two yesses; three noes, only one of which – concerning the ceding of a last, not quite uninhabited outpost of empire to a state itself notorious for a relaxed approach to human rights – required more than five minutes' contemplation.

When Margot returned to collect my decisions, I asked her what she likes doing when she's not at work. I wasn't expecting a real answer and was surprised to hear her say that she plays cards. I thought the young were all about video games and bungee jumps. (Clare never was, but that's another matter.) Margot said she played bridge at college, but now played poker, mostly, which surprised me even more.

I asked if she'd come across bezique. It's a two-player game I first learned from my grandfather when I was six. He told me with a wink that he'd taught himself to play it in a last-ditch attempt to woo my grandmother. I often think I might be the last afficionado left on earth. Predictably, Margot had never heard of it.

'You need two packs of cards,' I said, 'but you strip out all the 6's down. Tens rank between aces and kings – I've no idea why. There are loads of other quirks – like getting ten points just for having the seven of trumps – but mostly you score by matching cards into sets.'

'Like rummy?'

I would not allow my disappointment to show. It's a question every bezique-lover has heard a hundred times. Yes, the point is to make sets, or "melds", as they're known – sequences, marriages, quartets and, of course, beziques. But unlike rummy, melded cards can be reused in both tricks and future sets; and until the final eight tricks – when the stock is exhausted, and you're playing out your hand – you don't have to follow suit, or to win a trick if you can, which makes it so much harder to anticipate your opponent's moves. The result is an elaborate, demanding game of satisfying complexity: Dante to rummy's Betjeman, if you will; vintage Burgundy to rummy's plonk. If you've seen *The Apartment,* you'll know gin rummy just about makes Jack Lemmon sexy; bezique is an irresistible dance of the seven veils.

'What's a bezique?'

'It's where you pair up the Queen of Spades with the Jack of Diamonds. Sounds simple, but a double bezique – both Queens, both Jacks – is worth 500 points.'

Margot was intrigued.

I offered to teach her but didn't press the point. The freemasonry of the enthusiast has been established; it will not now be denied.

Before she left, I asked her for a DVD of *Passport to Pimlico.*

She smiled. Not a first, but the first time I'd detected more amusement than diplomacy in her expression.

'Nice try, Prime Minister.'

January 19th, Sunday

When I started, I thought I might write this diary every day, but I find the hours blend together seamlessly. I have ample time on my hands, but whole days pass by with nothing to distinguish them: so little snags the mind.

I knew I would miss the sky. I'm more surprised to find I miss the cold. That slight shudder when you leave the house and feel your skin retract, as if abraded. The pleasure of lying in a warm bed with your nose in the Arctic, or at least the Highlands. There are no windows here to open, and the air, constantly recycled, maintains an unwavering temperature and humidity that was initially comfortable but which I now find makes it harder and harder to sleep. The dermatitis that plagued me in the early years of my marriage has returned, spotting the Egyptian cotton when, inevitably, I scratch my own flesh raw. For exercise, I have one of those bicycles that propels you through a virtual landscape with a bewildering array of vital signs that would not disgrace an ICU. Who uses these things? Me, apparently. For another sixty-seven days.

The number of decisions has steadily increased. Margot says the Civil Service has geared up since the extended Christmas/New Year holidays; it will stay this way now until half-term. The mental effort required to determine my responses, however, remains low; I generally give Margot to believe the process takes far longer than it really does. It seems irresponsible, somehow, to despatch the daily business of the state in under half an hour.

In today's red box she brought, along with the usual dozen decision sheets, two packs of cards, still sealed. She did not mention them, however, and neither did I. Gerald never saw the point of games, and it has been some years since I played competitively; I wanted to remind myself of how the cards feel, how they behave, before we take the next step. Sharp as she is, Margot no doubt recognizes this.

Jan 23rd

Time passes, of course – what else would it do?

I watched the film adaptation of *The Collector*, with Terence Stamp. The blurb says it was nominated for three Oscars, but it lacked the impact I recall from reading the book, which Gerald pressed on me when we first met. He said he'd read it when it came out, when I would still have been a child. Perhaps it's me who isn't aging well?

Since then, I've watched *Brief Encounter*, *The Godfather II* (Gerald complained about Brando's mumbling through-out Part One) and *Key Largo* – because, well, Humphrey Bogart. Margot refused me *Casablanca*.

'Really?'

'I'm afraid so, Prime Minister.'

I've also taken the opportunity to re-read the kind of books I always told myself I would re-read. Not just Hardy: *A Passage to India*; some Henry James.

Only one decision today (apparently it is Sunday, but they're up against it on the legislative timetable). As a result of which many men will find themselves working considerably longer. It will do them no harm. Gerald should never have been allowed to retire at sixty. Not that his country deserved much more of him, perhaps. Then again, did I?

Jan 30th

Another Sunday. This morning, I cooked a proper lunch: roast chicken with stuffing and gravy, roast potatoes, carrots and broccoli, followed by an apple crumble with custard. Bird in the oven, I drank a glass of sherry and nibbled salted peanuts. Ridiculous, alone, I know: but why not?

This desire to cook is new, and something of a surprise. Outside, it had become a chore, all pleasure long since leached away. While Clare was growing up, Gerald demanded the same meals over and over again, the same seven dishes in the same order every week. Not a demand, he insisted, just a suggestion; he was trying to be helpful. It made sense, he said, with everything else I had on my plate ("no pun intended!") to minimize the time and effort wasted planning menus, shopping for new ingredients and cooking unfamiliar meals. Besides, didn't I always complain about having to decide what we would eat every week?

(It was true: I had complained.)

Clare also complained, of course: our food was boring; *we* were boring. We were so predictable. I couldn't help reflect that there is nothing more predictable than a teenager who complains about her parents. I kept the thought to myself. Gerald, however, said predictability was just another word for consistency, which was itself another way of saying *character*.

Clare said consistency betrayed a little mind.

By this time, I had moved to stand in front of the sideboard where we kept the better plates and glassware.

Gerald, torn between anger and pride, congratulated her on citing Emerson.

'Who's he?' said Clare. 'One of your old bosses when you had a job?'

I was glad that I had moved. But for once the air went out of Gerald.

When Clare returned from her first year at university, she informed us she was a vegetarian.

'Not a vegan, then?' said Gerald. 'You do know what happens to baby boy cows, don't you?'

Clare reserved the right to change her mind, but, in the meantime, discovered lactose intolerance, rendering the distinction almost moot. We ate a lot of free-range eggs that summer.

By the end of her second year, Clare weighed less than six stone and was allergic to both nuts and gluten. Tomatoes made her sick, and citrus made her sad. Gerald told her to pull herself together. I said she should see the GP. Clare rolled her eyes. I said Dr Pelly had known her since she was born, which didn't seem to make the prospect any more appealing. She went, though, in the end. Dr Pelly referred her to some adjunct of the mental health system which – eventually – signed her up to an online course of CBT. There were supposed to be six sessions, but Clare never got past the second. She didn't go back to university, either; and still hasn't. Gerald said if she thought she could just drop out, we weren't going to make allowances. I was to cook her whatever we were having. Whether she ate it or not was her affair.

That was a few years ago. Clare mostly makes her own food now and eats whatever she likes – which isn't much. She's doing better. Not so thin, anyway. Not so unremittingly angry. But when I got the call-up letter, she was outraged. She said no one should let me within a million miles of anything important. Which is the sort of thing I might have said myself, but Clare wasn't joking. I asked just what she meant and immediately regretted it.

She said I was as bad as him.

'Who?'

'*Who?* Listen to yourself. Dad.'

'Your father has . . .'

'Actually, you're worse. He's just ignorant. Or mad. He's got no idea. But you *know*. You know what he is. And still you go on, pretending everything's okay.'

I told her she didn't know what she was talking about. Her father was no longer himself.

'But he *is*, Mum. That's the trouble.'

She said I was an enabler. Like the people who buy drinks for alcoholics. Or guns for murderers.

I said I knew what an enabler was.

When I told Gerald I'd be away for three months, that I was going to be Prime Minister, he told me not to worry. He could look after himself, he said.

So, yes: roast chicken and all the trimmings. Sherry and a bottle of Chablis. Why in heaven's name not?

When I ordered the ingredients, Margot was too polite to raise an eyebrow. Without thinking, almost, I invited her to join me. I understand that this is work for her, but even so. You would think, once in a while?

She has her own family to consider, I expect. A husband; or at least a boyfriend.

She has, though, agreed to play bezique.

February 1st

The dermatitis has calmed down; the bed remains as comfortable as ever. I am even beginning to feel the benefit of the exercise bike.

Feb 11th

We have found that we are keenly matched. Margot is very clever but has an impetuous streak – it is her youth, I suppose – that lets her down as often as it precipitates a triumph. Of seven games, I have so far won four to Margot's three. Those three, it must be said, she did win by a country mile, while my victories have been narrow, dogged affairs. I am older; I am patient, and I am ahead.

Last night, having swept through my defences, she refilled our glasses and asked if I were enjoying my stint as Prime Minister. It is a topic we had previously avoided, despite our work here being the only thing we have in common, other than the cards.

I said it was a great deal easier than I'd expected.

'It doesn't give you nightmares?'

I laughed, certain she was joking. 'Am I doing it wrong?'

'Oh, no, Prime Minister.'

What else could she say?

'It's just – there's so little to do. We were always told PMs worked twenty hours a day. What on earth were they up to?'

Margot said the change had surprised the civil service, too, at first. After a while, though, it became clear that randomly selecting Ministers eliminated all the jostling for advantage, and with it the incentive to manage the news cycle.

'When you strip all that out,' she said, 'government is really pretty simple. There are so few decisions we really *need* you to take. Secretaries of State with no career ambitions send very little up to us at Number Ten. And then, Prime Minister, we find reducing every complex issue to a Yes/No question tends to make the answer obvious. Generally, decisions only make it to your desk when we need specific legal or constitutional authorisation.'

She was saying that I am, in fact, a rubber stamp. I thought of Gerald, in the years before he retired, railing about Ministers' inevitable stupidity. I said, 'It must be so much less fun for you?'

'We are here to serve, Prime Minister.'

I raised my glass in acknowledgment.

'We had one man,' she began, before checking herself. 'You must promise never to tell anyone I told you this?'

I took another mouthful of wine, gestured at the otherwise empty flat. Who could I tell?

'One man,' she repeated, 'asked what would happen if he refused to decide anything.'

I admitted I had wondered this myself.

'I said we would ask him to resign. He said he was Prime Minister: surely that would be his decision? Which, technically, it was. A bit of a cock-up in the drafting, if we're honest.'

Margot drained her glass, poured us both another.

'What happened?'

'We took him a decision form: would he resign – Yes or No?'

'And?'

'He refused to answer.'

'Hah!'

Margot leaned right forward, her bust disturbing the cards still laid out on the table. 'He said he was working to rule. Well, we said the rule was that we gave him decisions and he took them. In that case, he said, he was going on strike. For a week I brought his red box in the morning and in the evening took it away again – unopened. Eventually, we asked what his demands were. What would it take to settle this dispute?'

'And what did he say?'

Now she pushed her chair back from the table. She kicked off her shoes and stretched out one stockinged foot towards my knees, not quite making contact, before letting it drop. The gesture, perhaps unconscious, reminded me of Clare after all.

She said, "What would you have said?'

'I can have anything?'

'Within reason, Prime Minister.'

'I'd have asked you to pick Gerald after me. Then Clare. That way I'd have some peace and quiet when I get out.'

Margot cackled, and I feel terrible now, writing that down.

February 12th

I forgot to add, yesterday. Apparently, the striking PM's actual demand was that they abolish Sortition; that he should be the last. Margot told him they couldn't do that, not without another referendum. He demanded to decide there be a second vote. But we couldn't go back, Margot said. Nobody wanted that. Meanwhile, there was a bit of a backlog building up. The country wasn't exactly grinding to a halt, but there was more grit between the cogs than civil servants like. They had an important international summit coming up in a couple of months, and it was all getting a bit embarrassing. The UK would look ridiculous.

'Then, luckily,' Margot said, 'he got ill.'

Apparently, the rules allow for substitution in such circumstances. They just brought the next PM on early.

'Which is why you started when you did.'

So *that* explained the rush.

Also, Margot said, my stint would be a little longer than normal. Four months and four days. To get the cycle back on track.

No one had told me this, I said.

'Do you mind?'

I minded that no one had told me.

Feb 13th

Seventeen decisions; all yes.

After that, Margot explained how tomorrow's Summit will work. To maintain Purity, I cannot, of course, actually attend. Leaving No.10, travelling, conversation with fellow leaders, a formal dinner: far too much exposure to the political opinion of others. We couldn't have my future decisions contaminated by a few stray words from the German Chancellor or the President of the United States, now, could we?

Instead, I will attend by video link.

'I'll hear the debate, though?'

Apparently not. The video will be muted. I'll make a speech – a draft of which is working its way through final clearance now. A joint Foreign Office/No.10 team will feed me answers to any subsequent questions. None of which, Margot insists – apart from missing dinner and a much lower carbon footprint – is substantially different from the way such conferences were managed in the past.

In the middle of all this I mentioned that she had reminded me of Clare, which is only very slightly true. She shares Clare's instinctive desire for, and resistance to, physical comfort – the comfort, I mean, of another's touch, of touching another – but Clare lacks Margot's quickness, her wit and sly laughter. Really, the one she reminds me of is Gerald, when Gerald was her age and thought the world was there for him to take. How could I not love him, then? How can I not love him, now?

She did not respond.

Feb 14th, Valentine's Day

The Summit. My speech is incomprehensible to me even

as I read it. The Q&A involves red lines of some sort; also triple-sourced intelligence and territorial integrity.

Otherwise, I amuse myself by trying to read the lips and body language of my fellow world leaders. The Chinese president appears agitated, the Australian and Irish premiers, emollient. POTUS smiles a lot, but whether her smiles betray the teeth of a shark is hard to say.

Afterwards, Margot congratulates me. She has brought champagne. Why not, she says, it's so much cheaper after all than flying to Bahrain and back.

'Is that where I was?'

Feb 15th, 8.30 a.m.

Last night I lost to Margot at bezique. I lost: she did not beat me.

The champagne may have been to blame.

She started well – a favourable deal, an early sequence – but, as has become customary, I slowly ground my way towards victory. Having taken the lead with a ten-point trick, however, I felt a sudden urge to lead the Jack of Diamonds. A ridiculous move: I knew she had both the ten with which to win the trick and a Queen of Spades with which to pair the Jack for a bezique. I knew because both were face up on the table in front of her, constituent parts of previous melds. I played it anyway.

She seized the Jack and gleefully made her match. She said my head must have been spinning, turned by all the international glamour.

Who cared? It was only forty points.

Waiter! Another bottle!

Ten minutes later, the opportunity arose to repeat the move, but in reverse. I felt my stomach fall away, my heart leap heavenwards. In a flash, the second Queen was sacrificed, paired off with the second Jack for a double bezique. Five hundred points. Game over.

I had lost.

Margot feigned fury. To throw the game was sacrilege.

I said I was sorry.

She said it was insulting.

I said I couldn't help it; something had come over me.

She said I had to let her challenge me again, but this time it would be Rubicon.

She must have been doing her homework. Rubicon Bezique is a rarely-played, more refined and complex variant of the game; it requires 128 cards from four packs, and a mind like a steel trap.

I felt honour bound to accept.

As we did not have four packs at hand, however – and as we were by now both quite drunk – we agreed to play another day, shaking hands on the deal with stiff, exaggerated movements like court-martialled cavalry officers cutting off each other's epaulettes and buttons.

4.00 p.m.

What have we done?

Fourteen decisions today. All important, obviously, in their own way, but one a real headache, more powerful than my hangover.

They were brought to me in the usual red box by a young man with a long, narrow face and prominent knuckles. I asked where Margot was, hoped there was nothing wrong.

'I understand she is not well, Prime Minister.'

His tone managed to suggest that ill-health betrayed a feeble lack of grip, the sort of wishy-washiness one must expect in women.

I thought of all the champagne we'd drunk; thought also of my predecessor's convenient illness.

I placed the case on my desk and opened the lid. 'Thank you,' I said.

'Oliver, Prime Minister. Oliver Stratton.'

I hadn't been asking for his name.

When he left, I found the fourteen issues laid out as crisply as ever. Say what you like about the Senior Civil Service, Gerald used to say, it does wonders for a man's prose. Or a woman's, of course.

It was the eleventh that gave me pause. On my first day, before we got to know one another, Margot had made clear the very real threat of many more months' incarceration, in rather less comfortable accommodation, should I ever record, let alone reveal, the most secret contents of my red boxes. Decisions so classified, like this one, would be clearly marked. Suffice to say, then, that the future of the planet was at stake; or, at least, the future of a planet habitable by human beings. (Whenever Clare says we are destroying the world, Gerald delights in telling her not to be so anthropocentric: Earth will be just fine, he says.)

When Oliver returns, I ask for a little more time. When he returns again, I tell him to come back after lunch.

This one is not easy. Even boiled down: Yes, or No?

I think of Gerald, of how Gerald used to be. Of Clare.

Of going home when all this is over. Of what I might say when Gerald asks me how it was and doesn't listen to the answer; when Clare tells me what I should have done instead.

I think of Margot; of her apparent illness; of what, although she would never offer an opinion, she might say. The clasp of her hand as we shook on the deal.

Of what Oliver expects.

It is a formality, surely? Only here so the outcome bears my signature? A constitutional nicety.

Anyone would do.

With Oliver tapping at the door for the third time, I rummage in my handbag for a coin to toss.

Tolstoy's Mice

H E SAYS, 'I don't do that anymore.'
'I'm sorry,' she says. 'I wouldn't have asked. Only
. . . I'm sorry.'

Who is this apologetic woman at his door? Not literally
at the door, not now. He has invited her in, with a gesture
more than words. She is inside, in any case, in the kitchen.
He fills the kettle. Because that's what you do, isn't it?
When visitors call. It is what he does, although it has been
some time – two years at least – since there has been a
visitor here.

So, who is she?

Not a stranger, exactly, although they have never met.
He has seen her, many times, around the shops and on the
rec, between the pitches and the children's playground,
with the others. He has never wanted a dog himself. He has
witnessed their owners being dragged into conversation,
each dangling a small green plastic bag of lukewarm shit.
It's not the shit, it's the company he can live without.

She knows him, though. At least, she knows who he
used to be. The knock at his door was not random. Which
means he has a name, a name you might recognize, a claim

to fame. What passes for fame, here, in this village. So you might as well know that for more than thirty years – until a couple of years ago – his political cartoons appeared more or less daily in the pages of the national press, in leftish journals of one sort or another, and, latterly, on their websites, where the impact, he thinks, was much diminished. First the pages got smaller, then they became screens. Which wasn't a problem Gillray or Rowlandson ever had to face, now, was it? Then again, they couldn't finish a cartoon, then scan and upload it to the paper before lunch, all from a cottage in the country, could they? He was no Luddite, just tired.

She has come from the organizing committee, she says, from the community centre. The village is large enough, and wealthy enough, to support a community centre, along with three shops, a café and two pubs, one of which he visits frequently enough to be recognized as a regular. He has a usual pint there, and a usual table. He speaks to the bar staff, shares a few words with one of the other regulars, perhaps, before retreating to his table in the corner with a paper or a book. They were sorry to hear about his loss, the year before last. One or two of them remember his wife's parents, too, from years back. It is their house he lives in now; his wife's house; now his.

Who is she, again? This woman he has just handed a mug of tea? She must have a name. She has introduced herself, after all. All he caught was Beth; we will never know her second name. Short for Elizabeth he supposes, or possibly Bethan. A touch of Welsh, perhaps, in the way her intonation falls and rises? Or is he imagining it?

Beth says they're making posters, Facebook posts,

Twitter memes, you know the kind of thing. Drawing
attention to some injustice, some protest against injustice.
The committee thought perhaps one of his caricatures?
The Home Secretary perhaps? It would be up to him, of
course. It would catch the eye. Attract attention.

He has told her he doesn't do that anymore, but it
isn't entirely true. Each morning, after his walk around
the village, he sits at the huge drawing desk he has set
up in what was once his in-laws' bedroom, along with all
the paraphernalia of his trade. You can picture him for
yourselves, an old man curled in concentration among the
pencils, brushes and inks, the rulers and protractors and
other nameless geometric instruments you've had no use
for since you left school; the bright ungainly desk lamp
angled like a heron on a riverbank; newspaper cuttings and
inked-in scraps clipped to the edges of his steeply sloping
desk, or pinned to the walls, littering the floor; a framed
Hogarth sketch – a real one, not a print, a present from his
wife on their fortieth anniversary – which takes pride of
place, facing him, between the two windows that overlook
the garden, gone to seed now, and the new estate beyond.

Old? He is not so old as you might think. He's about the
same age as Beth, which is to say that they are both in their
sixties, although neither is yet eligible for a state pension.

Each morning, he starts several drawings, finishes at
least one. What he no longer does is sell them, or give them
away, even to good causes.

'It's not a protest,' Beth explains. 'It's a campaign to
support housing a refugee family in the village. We want
to show that refugees are welcome here.'

'And are they?'

'Of course.'

He'd like to think she's right, but there's no "of course" about it. If there were, the campaign would be unnecessary. He does not say so. It is not his fight.

Beth must have a motivation. Several, perhaps, but here's one she introduces at this point: her grandfather, of whom she was very fond, came here from Czechoslovakia in 1937, for the usual reason.

'Here to the village?'

'To England. London: Bethnal Green.'

'I lived in Bethnal Green for years.'

And there you have it – a point of connection. They could talk about the old East End; Brick Lane and Cable Street; Poplar and Shoreditch; Bloom's in Whitechapel, the Lahore Kebab Shop. They could share memories of the places, if not people, they both left long ago; but they don't. That is, she tries; he doesn't. He offers her a refill of tea. She confesses she does not know his work: she and her husband have *The Times* delivered.

'That's a relief,' he says. He couldn't abide a fan.

She has a husband, then? She has. Unlike his wife, her husband is not dead, but you must assume he is abroad, or professionally absorbed, or in some other way emotionally unavailable. She does not say so; not in so many words, but the clues are there, if he would only look. Nonetheless, this is the twenty-first century – even if the realization still sometimes surprises her – and if she does not have a flying car, she has at least had a job, a career, something in the line of good citizenship: a charity, perhaps, an NGO of which she became a director, in a sector where, even now, she sits on the boards of more than one organization you will have heard of. She is nobody's fool, least of all her own.

She asks to see some of his cartoons and he repeats that he does not do that anymore. It is still not true. He draws every morning, after his walk. It *is* true that the walk has lately become longer, or slower. It seems less and less important that he be at his desk at nine. All the same, he's there by ten, and for the next three hours or so. It is enough. If he did not draw, he does not know what he would do. It clears the mind. Afterwards, in the afternoons, he can read; in the evenings a glass of wine, or a pint in the pub, before supper. *Newsnight.* Sleep comes.

There must be five hundred finished pieces upstairs in his studio, his wife's parents' bedroom. He has never counted them.

'You must have some you could show me,' she says, 'from before you retired?'

He shakes his head. 'You won't want to see old cartoons.'

'I do,' she says.

He shakes his head again. 'There'd be no point,' he says.

She thanks him for the tea, apologizes again for troubling him. She asks him if – when they have a design – he would display one of their posters in his window. He does not say yes; but he does not say no, either.

Closing the door, he hears the soft pad of footsteps on the wooden stairs. It is nothing. His wife. Her dog. He puts on his coat and his cap and walks down through the village to the pub, carries a pint of the usual to his usual table.

What happens? Not much, to be honest. He's never been one for narrative. Single panels, not comic strips. There'll be no romantic encounter, not even a rueful epiphany regarding the opportunity he could not bring himself to seize. He is not unaware of her half-concealed invitation to start the whole business all over again, but the truth is, the truth – we cannot forego the word, even now – is that his lack of desire is real. It is not a mask for some vulnerability, some past wound. It cannot be ripped away, or lifted gently, tenderly, to allow a glimpse, or more, of new love. There is no self-deception here, no ironic distance between him and us. It is true. He has no desire to touch her, to talk to her, to discover her dreams and fears, or to share his own. He is not curious about the flesh beneath the clothes. He has not the energy to start all that again.

I have not the energy.

The following week, she shows him a copy of the final, amateurish, poster and asks him to display it. He agrees but lays it on the table as he makes a pot of tea. He does not lead her upstairs to see his studio. He does, however, tell her about a picture he once drew but never published.

'I called it "Tolstoy's Mice",' he says.

'Did Tolstoy have mice?'

In his *Confession*, he explains, Tolstoy tells the story of a traveller who hides in a dry well to escape a savage beast – only to find a dragon waiting at the bottom. 'I thought it would make a good cartoon,' he says. 'An allegory for something going on at the time. Half way down, the traveller grabs hold of a bush that's growing from a crack in the wall, then watches two mice, one white, one black, begin to gnaw away the roots. Whether he just lets go or waits for the mice to do their stuff, he'll wind up falling to the deadly dragon. Knowing this, he sees, on the leaves of the bush, some drops of honey, and licks them off. The question is: why? Why does he bother?'

'To enjoy the honey?'

'Ah, but he doesn't enjoy it. All he can think about is the dragon, the beast, and the mice, gnawing away. Why cling on? Why live?'

'Is it a riddle?'

'It's a confession, I'm afraid, so the answer is: God. It always is. But what if you aren't willing – or able – to suspend disbelief? What then?'

She has never believed, or felt the absence of belief. If the answer can be God, she thinks, it could just as well be love, or compassion, or humanity, even, but she does not say so.

He says, 'It's a trick, don't you see?'

She doesn't. She begins unobtrusively to gather her things.

'Like an optical illusion,' he says. 'All you need is a change of perspective. I realized this while drawing the mice. From the mice's point of view, it's obvious: they're there to supply the dragon with a steady diet of passing travellers.'

She thanks him for the tea, and says goodbye.

A day or two later, passing the house, she is surprised to see that he has put up the poster in his window.

Acknowledgements

I AM GRATEFUL to all those who organize, edit, publish and above all read the many magazines, websites and story competitions that, once in a while, make opening a writer's inbox so much more exciting. Earlier versions of stories collected here first appeared online or in print at:

Galley Beggar (*Confidence Interval*)
London Short Story Prize Anthology, 2018 (*the year of peace*)
Lunate (*The Long Hall*)
The London Independent Story Prize Anthology, 2023 (*Point and Shoot*)
The London Magazine (*Tolstoy's Mice*)

Thanks, too, to Chris and Jen at Salt, who have championed my writing over six books and more years than I care to remember.

This book has been typeset by
SALT PUBLISHING LIMITED
using Granjon, a font designed by George W. Jones
for the British branch of the Linotype
company in the United Kingdom. It has been
manufactured using Holmen Book Cream
65gsm paper, and printed and bound by Clays
Limited in Bungay, Suffolk, Great Britain.

CROMER
GREAT BRITAIN
MMXXVI